"I'm not getting married."

"I gathered that much," Jonah said dryly. "So what are you going to do instead?"

"I'm...leaving." Kathryn caught at his sleeve. "Please, I'm desperate. Will you help me?"

His eyes narrowed. "Tell me exactly what's in it for me."

She looked up at him and let her voice go sultry. "What do you want?" In a rush of gratitude, Kathryn said, "I'll give you anything you want...."

Leigh Michaels has always loved happy endings. Even when she was a child, if a book's conclusion didn't please her, she'd make up one of her own. And though she always wanted to write fiction, she very sensibly planned to earn her living as a newspaper reporter. That career didn't work out, however, and she found she ended up writing for Harlequin instead—in the kind of happy ending only a romance novelist could dream up!

Leigh likes to hear from her readers. You can write to her at P.O. Box 935, Ottumwa, Iowa 52501-0935, U.S.A. Or e-mail: leighmichael@franklin.lisco.net

Books by Leigh Michaels

BACKWARDS
HONEYMOON
Leigh Michaels

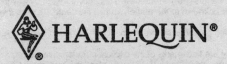

HARLEQUIN®

TORONTO • NEW YORK • LONDON
AMSTERDAM • PARIS • SYDNEY • HAMBURG
STOCKHOLM • ATHENS • TOKYO • MILAN • MADRID
PRAGUE • WARSAW • BUDAPEST • AUCKLAND

ISBN 0-373-03691-4

BACKWARDS HONEYMOON

First North American Publication 2002.

Copyright © 2001 by Leigh Michaels.

This edition published by arrangement with Harlequin Books S.A.

Visit us at www.eHarlequin.com

Printed in U.S.A.

CHAPTER ONE

STILL holding his comb, Antoine looked at Kathryn in the mirror and tugged at a glossy black curl until it descended to lie just right across the white lace shoulder of her gown. Frowning just a little, he stood back to study his client's hair once more, then reached for a spray bottle and began to mist the errant curl.

Kathryn stirred irritably. "Aren't you finished yet?"

"Have patience, mademoiselle. All must be perfection when you go to meet your bridegroom." Antoine snapped his fingers. "The headdress!"

An assistant sprang to attention and handed him a delicate wreath of orange blossom. Trailing from it, so delicate that it almost floated, was a floor-length veil edged with lace that matched that on the gown. As his skillful fingers pinned the wreath in place, Antoine murmured, "Mademoiselle is anxious for her wedding, yes?"

"Mademoiselle is anxious to have it over with," Kathryn said under her breath.

"Dear, dear." Antoine made a sort of clucking noise with his tongue as he inserted the last hairpin. "There. All is complete. Rest assured I will be waiting for you at the top of the stairs to make certain every hair is in place."

In that case, Kathryn thought, she should probably allow an extra half hour to get from her bedroom to the temporary altar set up in the ballroom downstairs.

Antoine's assistant started to gather up his tools, and

5

Kathryn's maid swooped down on her to make certain that the hairdresser hadn't put a nick in her makeup. Kathryn fended her off. "It's all right, Elsa. Go down to the kitchen, please, and bring me a cup of tea."

"I will call and have it brought up. Though I wish you wouldn't take the chance of spilling tea on that lovely gown, Miss Kathryn."

Kathryn's hands clenched on the edge of her dressing table. "All right, skip the tea." It took effort to keep her voice pleasant. "Just go away. After all the confusion, I'd like to have a few minutes to myself, Elsa."

"Of course, miss." The maid turned away, pausing to hold the door for the assistant.

He laid the last special comb in its fitted tray and picked up the heavy case. "Temper tantrums," he muttered to the maid as he passed her in the doorway. "All brides have 'em. Trust me. She's just excited at being so close to getting a wedding ring."

Kathryn rolled her eyes. *Excited* was hardly the word she'd have used to describe herself; *twitchy* was more like it. She supposed it was only natural to be on edge, after a full day of being poked and prodded and treated like a doll. And not the treasured porcelain kind, either, but the sort a small child dragged around by the arm and endlessly dressed and undressed...

At last the room was quiet. She stood up, automatically shaking out the full skirt of the satin and lace gown, but she didn't look at it in the mirror. Someone else would make sure, before she descended the stairs on her father's arm to meet Douglas in the ballroom for the ceremony, that each layer was perfectly arranged.

Kathryn didn't particularly care. She only wanted this

wedding—The Wedding of the Century, the newspapers were calling it—to be over.

It wasn't that she was having doubts, exactly. She'd made her choice logically, considering every possible factor before deciding that Douglas would make a suitable husband—and nothing had happened to change her mind about that. He was everything she'd looked for in a marital partner. Her father approved of him; Douglas was already an important cog in Jock Campbell's business. He was well-mannered and good-looking enough; he knew all the same people she did; he had never raised his hand or even his voice to her; and most important on Kathryn's list, he had enough money of his own that he didn't need to acquire hers.

No, she was certainly not having doubts about Douglas. It was simply the endless round of preparations that had worn her down.

Still, she reflected, going through all the motions of a formal wedding was little enough to do to please her father. If he wanted her to be the perfect June bride, then Kathryn would comply. And—incidentally—she would give him the means to pay back his social obligations to at least five hundred people by inviting them to her wedding.

Kathryn sighed. It wasn't like her to be so cynical. It must simply be that she was exhausted from the months of decisions and fittings and parties. But it would soon be over now.

She pushed open the French doors that led to the balcony and looked out cautiously. Her room was at the back of the house, and all the guests were supposed to be herded in through the front. But she was careful to stay close to the doors and away from the edge of the balcony, so no one could catch a glimpse of her even if they'd strayed out of place.

Even without hanging over the railing, though, she could at least take a deep, calming breath. It felt like the first one she'd managed all day. The air was unseasonably warm for northern Minnesota; if she'd realized that summer would come so early this year, she might have chosen a lighter weight of satin for her dress. Dancing in this costume was going to be—

The French doors of the room next to hers were open just a crack, and the murmur of masculine voices rubbed her nerves. Even on her own balcony she wasn't alone; apparently someone had assigned the next room for some of the ushers to use.

She tried to close out the sound, but the chatter which had surrounded her all day seemed to have sensitized her hearing; she couldn't help picking out words from the seemingly aimless conversation next door.

"And just in time, too," a man's voice said. "Another month and Doug would really have been on the ropes."

Kathryn heard only a murmur in answer; the speaker must have had his back toward the balcony doors.

"Yeah," the first man said. "He had to borrow the money from me to rent his tux because his credit cards are all maxed." Another murmur. "Because he's been on a losing streak, that's why. He was hoping that last trip to Vegas—you know, when he was supposed to be in San Diego schmoozing customers for Jock—would straighten him out so he might not have to go through with this after all. But instead he ended up owing the casinos, too, and you know how they are about collecting debts. If this wedding had been scheduled for next month instead, Miss Ice Cube Campbell might find herself marrying a guy with two broken knees.''

It can't be, Kathryn told herself. *They can't be talking about Douglas.*

But there was no one else they could have been speaking of. And there had been a flat, calm note in the usher's voice which convinced her he was speaking the truth— or at least giving the facts as he saw them. Still, he could simply be wrong, couldn't he? Perhaps he was misinterpreting what Douglas had said and done...

The hollow feeling in the pit of her stomach didn't go away.

She slipped back into her room and rang the bell for her maid. The few minutes that she waited for Elsa were the longest in Kathryn's memory.

Douglas, she thought. A gambler so compulsive that he saw a trip to Las Vegas as a way to pay off his previous bets? She'd always thought him a careful spender. A man so broke that he couldn't afford to rent a tux for his wedding? She'd seen him in formal clothes a number of times; it had never occurred to her that he might not own a tuxedo. A man so desperate...

That he'd lie and scheme to marry me, Kathryn thought.

Elsa tapped on the bedroom door and came in, looking hesitant. Kathryn gulped down her first instinct, which was to send Elsa shouting for Jock Campbell to come upstairs to his daughter *right now*. There was no sense in sending up an alarm, after all—and no one knew better than Kathryn how quickly a tasty bit of news could spread through the Campbell household. Let Elsa guess what was on her mind, and the butler, the gardener—

even the paperboy—would probably know it before Jock Campbell did.

"Please ask my father to come upstairs now," she said calmly.

Elsa looked confused. "But he's greeting the guests, Miss Kathryn. And there's still plenty of time before the wedding. You told me yourself that he'd be so sentimental about giving you away that you didn't want him to come up till you were ready to walk down the aisle—"

"I've changed my mind, and I'd like to spend a little time with my father. Please tell him that."

Elsa nodded and went out again.

Kathryn paced the floor. More than once her hand slipped under her veil to the back of her neck, to the top of the row of tiny satin-covered buttons which fastened the dress. Those fifty buttons running straight down her spine—the mark of a really professional dressmaker— had added a good bit to the price of her wedding gown. Now the irony was that she couldn't get out of the dress by herself....

She pulled herself up short. Exactly when, she wondered, had she decided that no matter what her father said, she was not going through with this wedding?

With a firm tap on the door, Jock Campbell poked his head in. "Is it safe?"

Kathryn turned to face him. "Daddy—" She bit her lip, not knowing what to say next. *Why* hadn't she thought this through before summoning him?

"How beautiful you are, my dear. As pretty as your mother, and that's saying a lot. Elsa seemed to think you were feeling a bit lonely up here. Wanted the old man's company, hmm?"

"I wanted to talk to you, yes. I'm…having second thoughts."

"About getting married? Oh, now, it's a little late for that, don't you think?"

"About Douglas, actually. Daddy…."

"Fine man, Douglas. Everything I could ask for in a son-in-law."

Kathryn took a deep breath. "You've never had any doubts at all about him?"

Was there a flicker of hesitation in his eyes? "No, dear," he said firmly. "And what you're suffering now isn't doubts, or even second thoughts. It's nerves, pure and simple. Your mother had them, too. She even sent for me, just minutes before our wedding was to start. Told me she wanted to call it off. She didn't, of course—and look how we turned out. Happy as clams for twenty-five years—and would be happy yet if it wasn't for…" His voice choked, as it always did when he referred to his wife's death.

Kathryn watched him strive for control. He had to work even harder at it than usual, but then this was an especially emotional day.

"Daddy," she said. "I'm really sorry to upset things, but this is not just nerves."

"Don't be ridiculous, Kathryn."

It was a rare day when she heard that stern note of finality in her father's voice, and something inside Kathryn curled up tight.

"Every bride has nerves," he said flatly. "If they all acted on the feeling, the institution of marriage would be extinct. I'm going downstairs to get Douglas, and after the two of you have talked, I will accept your apology for doubting my judgment in this matter, and then we'll go on with a wedding.''

''No!'' The word was out before Kathryn could even try to keep the panic out of her voice. She saw Jock's frown and said more quietly, ''No. Please don't bring him up here.''

''Are you afraid to face him, Kathryn?''

Yes. ''I… Of course not.'' She groped for an excuse, anything that might do. ''I just don't want him to see my dress before I get to the altar.''

How dumb can you be? she asked. She'd just neatly contradicted herself—saying one moment that she didn't want to proceed with the wedding at all, then the next proclaiming that the groom wasn't allowed to see the bride before the ceremony…

It was apparent that Jock Campbell hadn't missed the idiocy of the comment. He didn't even comment, just shook his head and went out.

Great job, Kathryn. Next time why don't you just stab yourself in the heart?

And now the clock was running. Jock would walk down the stairs at his normal relaxed pace, run his eye over the crowd to seek out his prospective son-in-law, pull Douglas aside in a casual way so as not to raise the concerns of the surrounding guests, and escort him upstairs. She had no more than twenty minutes, Kathryn estimated, before the two of them would be at her door.

She could already hear Douglas's smooth, patrician voice denying any misdeeds, claiming shock and surprise that anyone could make such an accusation. And what was she going to tell her father? That she chose to believe what she'd overheard from an usher rather than accept the reassurances of the man she was supposed to be trusting with her life?

She couldn't do it. She couldn't face down the two of them together. Which left only one alternative.

Kathryn tore open her closet, grabbed jeans, a pair of sneakers, and the first blouse her hand touched, and plunged into the bathroom. Putting both hands to the back of her neck, she clutched at the wedding gown, braced herself, and pulled hard. Buttons flew everywhere; for a moment the ceramic-tiled bathroom sounded like it was full of exploding popcorn.

She stepped out of the gown and wadded it up in the bathtub in order to leave herself enough room to step into her jeans. Tearing off her veil, she flung it over the door of the shower, then kicked off her white satin shoes and thrust her feet into the sneakers. Only then did she remember that she didn't have a cent on her, so—listening carefully for noises from the hall—she tiptoed back across the bedroom to where her honeymoon outfit was spread across the bed, dropped her engagement ring atop it, and grabbed the tiny evening purse that lay beside the dress. It was all she had time to take.

Still buttoning her blouse, she ducked back into the bathroom, pausing only to lock the door behind her, and went on through into the sitting room beyond. It opened into a secondary hall, around the corner from the main one which led to the grand staircase. There was no one in sight; she took the back staircase and peered around the corner at the bottom into the kitchen, breathing a sigh of relief when she saw it empty. All the employees must have already gone to stand at the back of the ballroom in order to watch the ceremony.

A ceremony which was not going to happen.

Kathryn paused for a moment outside the back door, then headed for cover behind the nearest large tree and started to work her way across the garden trunk by trunk. Her plan was so simple it could be summed up in two words: *Get away*. She didn't care where, and she didn't care how.

Her heartbeat slowed a bit as she increased her distance from the house, and with the first hurdle behind her, she turned her attention to figuring out how to get off the estate. Jock Campbell's big Georgian-style house didn't look a bit like a moated castle, but with its high brick walls and iron gates it was nearly as impregnable.

And getting out wasn't much easier than getting in—especially today, when the guards would be extra alert in order to secure all the wedding gifts on the premises, to say nothing of protecting five hundred guests who were all wearing their best jewelry. And in a very few minutes, as soon as Jock discovered her abandoned wedding gown, it would become even more difficult to circumvent the security arrangements.

She was chewing on that, trying to figure out the weak spot in her father's defenses, when she popped out from behind a hedge into the narrow driveway beside the gardener's cottage and tripped over a pair of legs sticking out from under an old car.

A growl came from underneath, and a body, lying on a rolling board, slid into sight.

''What the hell—''

Kathryn's gaze slid slowly from the man's dirt-splotched sneakers past a pair of jeans so worn that they were barely blue and across a grease-smeared T-shirt. She focused on a pair of broad shoulders, a tanned, rugged-looking face, a thatch of unruly dark hair, and a pair of deep brown eyes that snapped with aggravation.

"Can't you watch where you're walking?" he grumbled.

"Sorry. I was thinking."

"Oh, you're one of those people who can't walk and think at the same time." He sat up, and suddenly his gaze sharpened. "You're supposed to be getting married just about now."

Kathryn looked through him. "You must have mistaken me for someone else."

"Really? Then what's that bit of orange blossom doing stuck in your hair?"

Her fingers found the stray petals and plucked them loose, then began to seek out hairpins, destroying the formal hairstyle Antoine had worked so hard to produce.

"Katie Mae Campbell in the flesh," the man mused.

Kathryn bristled. "Nobody has called me that since I was six years old, and I do not plan to make an exception anytime soon. Miss Campbell will do. Or, if you insist, you can call me Miss Kathryn."

"And as I'm saying it, I should pull my forelock respectfully like a good peasant, I suppose." He rose slowly, with a panther's grace, and reached for a rag lying on the car's fender to wipe his hands.

He was taller than she'd thought; Kathryn found herself looking a long way up. "Who are you, anyway?"

"Jonah Clarke. My father is your gardener, in case you don't know."

"Of course I know his name. That explains why you recognized orange blossom from seeing a single petal."

"He'd be proud of me. Also he'd be charmed that you came to visit, only he's not here. He's over at the big house to attend your wedding. Which sort of brings us back to where we started.''

It was none of his business, of course. ''Why aren't you with him?'' The question wasn't entirely a delaying tactic; Kathryn was honestly curious.

''I wasn't invited. I'm only here to visit him for the day.'' He tossed the rag aside. ''So tell me, *Miss Kathryn*—what gives?''

''I'm not getting married.''

''I gathered that much,'' he said dryly. ''So what are you going to do instead?''

''I'm...leaving.''

''I see. Well, if you're looking for your Porsche, I think the garage is still on the other side of the property.''

She bit her lip and looked at him, debating. She was down to minutes, if even that long, before the alarm went up, and standing here talking was getting her nowhere at all.

''Jonah,'' she began. ''You know perfectly well that I—''

''Mr. Clarke will do.'' He mimicked her tone. ''Or, if you insist, you can call me...well, let's stick to Mr. Clarke. It's much tidier.''

''Mr. Clarke,'' she said firmly. ''You grew up here on the estate, am I right?''

He nodded. He looked wary, she thought.

''Then you must know if there's any way out of this place other than through the front gates.''

He raised an eyebrow. ''You don't even know me, but you're assuming that I was the sort who would go sneaking out over the walls at night.''

''Well, didn't you?''

He grinned. "Of course I did."

"How?"

"Oh, no. I'm not telling you."

She caught at his sleeve. "Please," she said. "I'm desperate, here. I have to get outside these walls, right now. Will you help me?"

His eyes narrowed. "Tell me exactly what's in it for me—besides a whole lot of grief when your dad catches up with me—and I'll consider it."

She looked up at him and let her voice go sultry. "What do you want?"

"What are you offer—" He broke off and shrugged. "Oh, forget it. Katie Mae, you are too dangerous to be let loose on the world."

"I told you not to call me—" She paused. "Come to think of it, you can call me anything you want to if you'll just help me get over the wall."

"Will going through it be good enough?" He pushed open the side door of the garage and leaned into the dark interior. Then he dangled a large, old-fashioned key in front of her.

In a rush of gratitude, Kathryn said, "I'll give you anything you want."

"I'll think it over and let you know. Come on."

His loose-limbed stride ate up the ground; Kathryn had trouble keeping up with him as he plunged deeper into the woods which filled a good part of the Campbell estate.

"So where are you headed?" he asked over his shoulder.

"You don't think I'd tell you, surely."

"That probably means you don't know."

"No, it means I expect you'd turn around and sell the information to my father."

"Sure I will. I'll march right up to him and say, 'Jock, old buddy, I can tell you where your daughter went, and I know because she confided in me while I was hoisting her over the wall.' I'm sure he'd reward me, probably right after he slugged me in the face."

"What about the key? I thought that meant there was a door or something."

"You don't think I'd tell him all my secrets, do you? He'd have it sealed up in a minute, and who knows—I might want it again someday."

"Thinking of moving back in with your father, are you?" she asked sweetly.

"It wouldn't be my first choice, but you never know what might come up." He stopped abruptly. "Here."

Kathryn could see the vine-shrouded wall beyond the last row of trees, but she couldn't see anything that resembled a gate or a door. "Where?"

"Good disguise, isn't it?" he said cheerfully. "The vines were here when I found this place, but it took me a couple of years to train them just right so they'd hide the door without breaking when it was opened. Let's see if they still do." He pulled back a curtaining vine to reveal an arch-topped door built of heavy planks.

The key slid silently into place and the lock opened with a discreet click. On the other side of the thick wall hung another curtain of vines. Kathryn ducked underneath it and looked out across an expanse of pine woods that spread downhill as far as she could see, full of undergrowth and brambles. She looked uncertainly out across the dappled hillside. "Um…where am I?"

"Some Boy Scout you'd make. About five hundred yards through there is the state highway."

She bit her lip. "I suppose once I get there I could hitchhike."

"I'd suggest you hurry, or you'll probably be trying to thumb a ride with some of your own wedding guests."

She looked up at him through her lashes. "Maybe you should come with me."

He said something under his breath. She was rather glad she hadn't heard it clearly.

"Jonah... I mean, Mr. Clarke...you won't ever be able to collect whatever I owe you for helping me escape, if you don't know where I went."

The silence stretched out endlessly.

"One thing's certain," he muttered. "It's becoming obvious that I like pain. All right, I'm in for the adventure."

She smiled in triumph. "Then let's lock the gate and get going."

Jonah shook his head. "Not so fast. I may be a masochist, but I'm not an idiot. I was checked into the estate on the guards' list this morning. If I'm not checked out the same way, all hell will break loose and they'll be looking for both of us."

"Oh. I hadn't thought of that."

"Along with half a million other things you haven't considered, I'll bet. Anyway, I don't fancy being shot at by the FBI because they think I'm holding you hostage."

"Why would they think that?"

"Did anyone see you leaving?"

She shook her head.

"Did you tell anybody you were going?"

"Not exactly."

"Then they have no way of knowing if this stunt was your idea or someone else's. Look, we haven't got time to argue. You take off through the trees—just walk toward the sunset and you'll come out near a little roadside park. I'm going to go back in, get my car, and leave just as I normally would. I'll probably beat you to the park, but if I'm not there, hang around back in the trees till I show up." He pulled the vines back and stepped into the wall.

"Jonah," she said softly, and he turned. "Thank you."

"Don't thank me until we've gotten somewhere." A moment later the door closed with a creak and he was gone.

Kathryn walked as fast as she could, aiming for the brilliant sliver which was all she could see of the sun. It seemed to be sinking faster than it ever had before. She didn't want to think about what would happen if darkness fell while she was still in the woods. She didn't think the small vial of pepper spray which she always carried in even the smallest handbag would be much help at all against a bear or a cougar or any of Minnesota's other wildlife.

But before she realized that the pine woods had been gradually thinning, she stumbled out of the shadows and found herself at the edge of a park so tiny it was nothing more than a U-shaped lane with a picnic table and a garbage can. It wasn't as late as she had feared; now that she was out of the woods she could see that the sun was only starting to drop below the horizon.

Parked in the lane was the old car Jonah Clarke had been working on in his father's driveway, and Jonah was leaning over the picnic table with a map spread out in front of him. She saw that he'd stopped long enough to change his greasy T-shirt for a pullover that matched his eyes.

Kathryn almost ran the last few steps. "You're a marvel! How did you know I'd come out exactly here?"

He looked up from the map. "Considering that it was you doing the navigating, it was nothing more than a lucky guess. I was starting to wonder if you'd had second thoughts and decided to just follow the wall around to the front gates instead."

She shook her head firmly. "And leave you waiting here, wondering what happened to me?"

"It was a pleasant daydream, anyway," Jonah mused. "Come on, let's get going. Want a sandwich?"

"No, thank you—but if you have some water I wouldn't turn it down."

"In the car."

She slid into the passenger seat and he handed her a bottle of spring water. She took a long, satisfying swallow.

He'd started the engine but made no move to put the car into gear.

"Where are we going?" Kathryn asked.

"Well, it sort of depends on what you want to accomplish. But since there's nothing north of here but the Canadian border—"

"I have my passport," she said brightly.

He stared at her. "You leave home with nothing except the clothes you're wearing but you take a *passport?*"

"Well, not deliberately. I mean, I didn't consciously think about leaving the country. But Douglas was going to take me to Bermuda for our honeymoon, so of course my passport was in my handbag." She dangled the tiny purse in front of him and thought, *I wonder how Douglas intended to pay for Bermuda. Or was he expecting that I would?*

Jonah grunted. "Nevertheless, I think we'll go south. It's three hours to the Twin Cities, so you'll have plenty of time to tell me what you're planning to do."

I'll do that. Just as soon as I figure it out myself. "Three hours? It never takes me that long to get to the Cities."

"That's because you take the main highway, which is exactly the first place they'd look for us."

"Oh. I hadn't thought of that."

He shot a sideways look at her. "There's obviously a good deal you haven't thought about, Katie Mae."

"I guess I'm really lucky you decided to come along," she admitted. "For one thing, they'll be looking for a woman alone, not a couple. It's perfect."

"Perfect? That's one possible point of view. Not necessarily mine. You can start by telling me what prompted this sudden decision to leave home. At least, I hope you aren't going to tell me you've been planning this escape for weeks."

The dry note in his voice made her smile a little. "No, it was quite sudden. What it boils down to is that I found out just this afternoon that Douglas didn't want to marry me, but he desperately needed my money." Despite her best efforts, her voice quivered just a little. Putting it into words, admitting what a gullible fool she'd been, didn't come easily.

"Your father's money, you mean."

"No, my money," she corrected. "When Daddy incorporated his restaurant chain and started selling franchises to people all over the country who wanted to run Katie Mae's Kitchens, he put thirty percent of the company in my name."

"And you were how old then?"

Kathryn considered. "Three. Maybe four."

"Great idea. A major stockholder who can't spell *kitchen*, much less know her way around one."

She decided to ignore him. "At any rate, Douglas was forcing himself to marry me so he could use my money to pay off his gambling debts."

There was a long silence. "You made a good decision," Jonah said gruffly.

"I'm glad you approve."

"To dump him, I mean. Running away…well, that's not so smart. Why didn't you tell your father what you'd found out? Kick the jerk out and then go right on and dance at your party?"

"I tried," she said softly.

"Jock didn't believe you?"

"He trusts Douglas. Just as I did."

The hiss of the tires on the highway mingled with the throaty hum of the engine to produce a hypnotic murmur. The strain of the day gradually began to melt out of Kathryn's body, to be replaced by exhausted acceptance.

"I never thought Douglas loved me," she said, almost to herself. "That was all right, because I didn't exactly love him, either. But I thought he respected me. Liked me. To find out that he didn't…that it was just the money again…."

"Again?"

She nodded. "All my life people have been more interested in my money than in me. But it never went this far before. The others weren't as good as Douglas at covering things up, so it didn't take as long to discover the truth—that a man who was admiring my every habit and hanging on each word was really eyeing my bank balance instead."

"It's happened a lot, then."

She sighed. "It seems like just about everybody I ever dated. I think that was one of the reasons I wanted to marry Douglas—so it would all be over and I wouldn't have to guard against fortune hunters anymore."

"Well, now's your chance to get away from them. A once-in-a-lifetime opportunity."

"Yeah," she said softly, and turned to face him. "You're right. Once in a lifetime." She took a deep breath. "Jonah Clarke, will you marry me?"

CHAPTER TWO

JONAH'S hand jerked on the steering wheel and the car swerved across the center line and halfway into the oncoming lane. He pulled it firmly back to safety and reminded himself that no matter what kind of kooky question his passenger asked, it was no excuse to take his attention off the road even for an instant.

"It's fortunate that eighteen-wheeler wasn't any closer," Kathryn said coolly.

Almost automatically, Jonah defended himself. "It was a good quarter of a mile away."

"And closing fast. What's the matter, did I shock you?"

"You could say that. What the hell are you talking about, asking if I'll marry you?"

She shifted her shoulder belt and wriggled a little. "I thought the question was pretty clear, myself. What didn't you understand?"

"For one thing, how you got from having a once-in-a-lifetime opportunity to dump the fortune hunters to issuing a marriage proposal."

Kathryn shrugged. "It wasn't much of a leap. I just figured you were thinking along the same lines."

"Me?" Jonah knew he sounded appalled, and he didn't care. "I was suggesting that the rich little girl who attracts all the riffraff could disappear right now. You could go somewhere new and just be plain Kathryn Campbell instead, and then you'd be sure that any man who came buzzing around you wasn't after the money, because he wouldn't know about it.''

''Would I be sure?'' she asked, sounding almost wistful. ''How could I ever be certain that he hadn't done some secret research?''

She had a point, Jonah supposed. There were lots of ways to find people's secrets, and anyone who was interested in marrying money would certainly know how to sniff out the details. ''So change your name. If you'd go wait tables at a Katie Mae's for a while, you'd soon learn to tell who was serious and who wasn't.''

''Hide out in my father's own restaurant chain?''

''He certainly wouldn't be looking for you there. But I suppose you couldn't live without your luxuries for longer than a day or two, and it would be more difficult to conceal your financial circumstances if you were driving a Porsche and wearing designer suits.''

''How much do you want to bet that I can't do without all the luxuries? Besides, I don't own a Porsche, I've never owned a Porsche, and I don't intend to own—''

''Then no doubt you prefer Jaguars. Don't change the subject, Katie. What the devil were you thinking, asking me a question like that? Or do you ask every man you meet to marry you?''

''Don't be silly. I only thought that you might be... well, everybody could use a little extra money, right?''

''I suppose so,'' Jonah admitted. ''But—''

''So I thought we could make some sort of a deal. I do owe you, you know.''

''You said I could have my choice, remember?'' He frowned. ''You can't actually be serious. Because I think I heard you say that you'd pay me to marry you, in order to avoid being chased for your money—and that makes no sense at all.''

"Yes, it does. It would be clean and up front, with no sneaking and no lying." She looked out the window. "Oh, just forget it."

He'd like to forget it. But the question she'd asked was still echoing through his mind. Along with it circled something else she'd said, in that wistful way of hers: *That was one of the reasons I wanted to marry Douglas, so it would all be over and I wouldn't have to guard against fortune hunters anymore.*

Now he could see the convoluted, Katie-Mae-Campbell sort of logic in the plan. It ranked right up there with her escape stunt.

"You're saying that you'd rather marry an honest fortune hunter," he said slowly, "than one who's trying to hide himself behind a pretense of loving you."

"At least I'd know the truth. Really know it, not just suspect." To his surprise, there was no defensiveness in her voice, only a note of sadness. "And knowing up front would be a lot better than being made to feel like a fool in the end."

At that instant, Jonah wanted—more than anything else in the world—to be able to wipe her unhappiness away. But that, he told himself severely, was clearly not one of his saner impulses.

"So what will you do next?" he asked casually.

"Now that you've turned me down? I don't know. Probably look for someone else who likes the deal better."

The woman was completely self-destructive. How she had managed to make it this far was beyond him. Out on her own, alone in the world—she'd be shark bait, no question about it. But even worse, she was actually going to invite the sharks to come closer and circle around....

He took a deep breath and tried to look at things from her perspective. Her nickname was a byword across the nation. Her picture—actually it was a photo of her as a child, but there was no question the resemblance was still a strong one—was a trademarked symbol. How could she ever be absolutely certain that any man loved her for herself and not her money?

"How did you decide on Douglas?" he asked.

For a moment he thought she wasn't going to answer. "His family mined iron ore in the Mesabi Range. Only instead of reinvesting everything in iron, they bought banks. His share of the family wealth should have been worth a whole lot more than my thirty percent of Katie Mae's Kitchens."

"Ah," he said on a note of discovery. "So you were something of a fortune hunter yourself!"

"I thought someone who had his own money wouldn't be particularly interested in collecting more. Obviously it wasn't a workable plan, so I'll try something else." She was staring straight ahead as she said softly, "I'm going to marry somebody. I'd much rather it be you, Jonah."

"I'm not sure that's a compliment," Jonah said dryly. "You don't know anything about me."

She shot a glance at him. "So what? I knew an awful lot about Douglas. Probably just about everything there was to know—except for the gambling debts."

"I take an occasional five-dollar flyer on a sports pool," he warned.

Kathryn shrugged. "Big deal. Besides, I know the important things. I know your father. I know you grew up on the estate.''

''If you think that makes us similar, take another look. There's a great deal of distance between the big house and the gardener's cottage.''

''Of course there is. But just because you were there, you can understand—more than anyone else can—how it was for me, growing up there.''

He cast his mind back over the years. Not that he'd seen her often—and perhaps that was the point she was trying to make. Katie Mae Campbell had not only been isolated by walls and gates, but by her social status. Even the few other children who lived on the Campbell estate had been discouraged from making any contact with her. Jonah himself had never tried; the few times he'd encountered little Katie Mae had been completely accidental. But then he'd been half a dozen years older and much too mature—in his own estimation, at least—to be interested in a little girl with glossy black curls and wide, dark blue eyes. A girl who was always dressed in ruffles and who looked as if she'd never dream of climbing a tree.

How lonely she must have been, he thought.

''Your parents meant well,'' he said. ''Keeping you protected like that. After that kidnaping threat—''

''I know they had to protect me.'' The resignation in her voice abruptly gave way to something like triumph. ''See? You *do* understand how it was.''

''A little, maybe.''

''And I know that you're kind,'' she said softly, ''or you wouldn't have helped me get outside the walls in the first place. Very kind, or you wouldn't be helping me right now.''

Lunatic, he thought, would be a more accurate description.

He let the silence lengthen and finally said, "I think we should find a pay phone so you can call your father. At least let him know you're safe."

She laughed. "And you talk about *me* not being logical?"

"If you didn't even leave a note—"

"There wasn't time."

"He'll be worried about you."

"Jonah, that place is so wired for sound that he could trace me within fifteen seconds of answering the phone."

"He has good reason for that. And maybe I can figure a way to get around it."

"If you can do that, you're the greatest electronics genius of your day. Even twenty years ago, he had a good enough bugging system that—" Her voice caught.

Jonah nodded. "That he told the FBI precisely where to find the extortionists who'd phoned him and threatened to snatch you if he didn't pay them off. I remember. That incident is exactly why you shouldn't leave him in suspense this time."

"The system is a whole lot more sensitive now."

"I'll figure something out—at least a way to get a message to him. He's not young anymore, Katie. Don't make him suffer unnecessary stress."

"Who are you, anyway? His doctor?" She sighed. "All right, but it's on your head. If your great idea fails and he finds me, I'm holding you responsible."

"Maybe he'll be so glad to hear from you that you'll be headed straight home of your own free will."

She didn't answer that, but the tilt of her eyebrows

spoke volumes. A little later, she said, "This deal we've been talking over—what about if I offer you fifteen percent of Katie Mae's Kitchens?"

"Fifteen percent of the company or fifteen percent of your share? Not that I'm indicating interest either way, you understand. It's just idle curiosity."

She looked at him sideways. "Oh, sure, you're just curious. I meant of the company. That leaves me fifteen percent. My father still holds forty and the rest of the shares are owned by a bunch of investors, so it wouldn't change anything, really. I'd still be a major stockholder."

Jonah shook his head. "You need to learn to negotiate, Katie. Pick your man carefully, approach him right, and you could probably settle for five percent. Certainly for ten."

She raised her chin a fraction. "I'd rather be fair up front and get things settled quickly."

Shark bait, he thought. *She's doomed.*

Fifteen minutes later, Jonah slowed for a small town. "I wonder if there's a library here."

"Probably not one that's open at this hour on a Saturday night. What do you want to look up, anyway?"

"Libraries have public-access computers, sweetheart. If nothing else, we can send your father an e-mail. He does have an e-mail address, doesn't he?"

"Oh, yes. His newest toy is a gadget the size of a remote control that lets him download his mail anywhere. He's in love with that thing. But can't e-mail messages be traced?"

"Not this one. Not by the time I get done with it."

"In that case, there's an easier solution." She pointed at a low building across the highway.

"A coffeehouse?"

"Look at the neon sign in the window."

"Internet access. Perfect." He swung the car into the parking lot.

The coffeehouse wasn't particularly busy, but Jonah guided Kathryn to a booth instead of toward the row of computers along one side of the room. When she gave him a questioning look, he said, "I could use a cup of coffee. Besides, we'd be more likely to be noticed if we went straight for the computer. Noticed—and remembered, in case anyone happens to come along and ask. What would you like?"

"Whatever you're getting for yourself."

"I'm ordering a large, plain, house blend—black, no sugar. If you'd rather have something fancy—"

Kathryn shook her head. "I wish you'd get over this idea that I only like something if it's expensive and exotic."

He gave the order to the waitress and added casually, "By the way, what's special about the computer in the corner over there? The one that has its own little room?"

The waitress looked over her shoulder as if she wasn't sure which one he meant. "It's wired for sound," she said. "We've got some customers who can't type, so they like that one. They can just talk to it."

Jonah summoned his best smile. "Can you put me on the waiting list to use it?"

The waitress blinked and gulped. "I'll make sure you're next."

He turned back to find Kathryn looking at him thoughtfully.

"Don't start talking about your bargain here," he said.

"I wasn't planning to. I do have some discretion. I also am capable of feeling shame, which you obviously aren't. Flirting with the waitress like that—"

He was mildly indignant. "I didn't hurt her in the process of getting what I wanted."

"Maybe not, but she's going to be hanging around staring at you and soaking up every word you say as long as you sit here. If you didn't want to be noticed—and remembered—you've gone about it exactly wrong."

Their coffee arrived at breakneck speed, and the waitress confided, "The guy who's using the computer now is in here every night, so I told him his time was up in five minutes."

"Thanks," Jonah said.

Kathryn only raised her eyebrows and sipped her coffee.

Once they were in the enclosed booth, it took him hardly any time at all to set up the Internet connection so it would operate like a regular telephone. "Here." He handed the headset microphone to Kathryn. "You talk in here, but your father's voice will come out of the speakers."

She hesitated. "And you're certain he won't know where I'm calling from?"

"If his system can figure out anything at all—which I doubt—it'll tell him you're in Seattle. Go on, dial the phone."

She clicked out the number of Jock Campbell's private phone line on the screen display, and just moments later heard her father's voice. "Daddy?"

"Kathryn! Thank God. Where are you, darling? Are you all right?"

"I'm fine, Daddy."

"And you're coming straight home, aren't you? Douglas is here with me. He's upset, of course, and he doesn't understand why you left anymore than I do, but he's quite willing to let bygones be bygones."

Kathryn shot a look up at Jonah, who had perched on the arm of her chair. "So he's willing to marry me even though I ran away?"

"Of course he is, darling."

In the background she heard an Ivy League accent. "Tell her we've both made mistakes. Of course I'll forgive her."

"Well, that's too bad for him," Kathryn said crisply, "because I'm not willing to forgive his. You might ask him about his last trip to Las Vegas, Daddy—the one when he was supposed to be somewhere else. And while you're at it, you might take a really careful look at Douglas's finances."

Jock sounded puzzled. "What was that, Kathryn? I only heard part of that. Your voice was breaking up, as if there was some electronic interference."

Jonah muttered, "Hang up."

"Is there someone there with you, darling?" Jock's voice sharpened into suspicion. "Is someone telling you what to say?"

"No, Daddy. I just called to tell you not to worry about me. But I won't be coming home for a while."

"Kathryn—"

She clicked the disconnect button and turned to Jonah. "There. I tried to be reasonable. Are you satisfied?"

He nodded absently. He was thinking hard.

"Good." She led the way back to their booth. "Now that I've set Daddy's mind at rest—so to speak—what's next?"

He took a long swallow of coffee. "What else do you have in that purse besides a passport?"

"Credit card. Makeup. Nail file. That kind of thing."

It figured, he thought. She carried everything she considered essential, but not much that was useful. "Any actual money?"

"Not much. I've never been in the habit of carrying cash."

He supposed that for most of her life she hadn't needed to. There would have always been someone with her to pay the bill or sign the charge ticket. "That's too bad, because I don't have a lot on me at the moment, either. Your credit card accounts are probably already being watched, so if there's a transaction, Jock will know it before the ink's dry. I've got a card, too, but it won't be good for much longer, either."

"Why not? Nobody knows you're with me."

"Jock will know soon enough, honey. They'll be questioning everybody who was on the estate today. And when they find out that I left about the same time you did, and that nobody's seen me since.... Well, it never did take Jock Campbell long to add two and two and come up with half a dozen. We are going to need to get hold of some serious cash."

"Why?"

"Because we're going to be on the run for a while. I wish the library was open."

She frowned a little and said very gently, as if she was humoring him, "If you're thinking of somewhere to rob, wouldn't it be better to choose a bank?"

"Thank you for that excellent advice, Katie Mae," he said dryly. "I'm not planning to steal the overdue book fines, I want some information—because at the moment,

I don't know how far we'll have to go, or even in what direction.''

"For what?'' She was beginning to sound exasperated.

"To find a state…'' he set his coffee cup down with a firm click and looked at her very deliberately "…where we won't have to jump through a lot of hoops in order to get married.''

Kathryn choked on a mouthful of coffee. "You mean…you…''

"I'll marry you, yes. Or are you backing out of the deal?''

Am I? She'd have expected to feel relief at his announcement, not this sudden wave of blinding panic. This was what she'd wanted, she told herself desperately. What she'd asked for. But now…

It's just the suddenness of it, she told herself. *It's the same good idea it always was. I'm just surprised that he changed his mind, that's all.*

Of course, said a little voice in the back of her brain, *fifteen percent of a national restaurant chain was well worth changing one's mind for.*

But wasn't that the whole point? She knew exactly why he was marrying her; that absolute certainty was why she'd made the offer in the first place.

"No,'' she said as firmly as she could manage. "I'm not backing out.''

"Then from here on out, we're partners. Fifty-fifty in everything, right?'' He held out a hand.

She laid her palm against his and felt an almost electrical zing from the contact.

"What am I thinking? I don't need a library,'' he

muttered, and only an instant after taking her hand, he pulled away. Before Kathryn could gather her wits, he'd crossed the room again to a vacant computer station.

She sipped her coffee. It was cold now, but she didn't care.

Married. She could almost hear her father roaring at the news that within hours of her broken engagement she was seriously planning to marry a different man.

A very different man, she thought. With Jonah, there were no false promises, no crossed fingers behind the back, no faked declarations of love. Just honesty and openness. And kindness, of course. Perhaps that was the most important factor of all, in Kathryn's estimation. Few men would brave Jock Campbell's wrath in order to help his daughter, even with the promise of a good chunk of his empire dangling before them. Jonah—despite his firsthand experience of what the man was capable of—hadn't hesitated. And he'd done a good deal of helping even before she'd offered him the deal of a lifetime.

Well, Kathryn corrected, he hadn't hesitated *much.*

Jonah came back to the table, folding a paper napkin. "This may be a little trickier than I thought. It appears that the easiest places to get married in this country are a long way from Minnesota."

"Well, putting some distance between us and my father might not be a bad idea."

"A *very* long way. We don't have enough cash to buy airline tickets, and if we used a credit card, Jock would know about it long before we reached our destination."

"He'd probably be waiting for us in the terminal," Kathryn agreed.

"So it needs to be somewhere within driving distance.

However, as far as I can determine, every state around here requires either a waiting period or blood tests or both.''

''I can see why you'd object to the waiting period,'' Kathryn said reasonably, ''but what's wrong with blood tests? Are you afraid of needles or something?''

Jonah shook his head. ''It's the uncertain time element that bothers me. It can take days to get a lab report, maybe even longer than the official waiting periods are. And the more time we stay in one place—''

''The more likely it is that Daddy will catch up with us.''

''Of course, he can't really prevent you from doing anything you want,'' Jonah pointed out. ''You're an adult and you can marry whomever you choose, even if Jock's standing right there yelling at you about it.''

Kathryn made a face. ''Not a pretty picture. I think I'd rather present him with a *fait accompli*.''

''That's what I expected you to say. So the best choice I've found is Nevada.''

''Las Vegas?'' She was horrified.

''What's wrong with it?''

She bit her lip. ''I guess it's a silly objection, but apparently it's one of Douglas's favorite playgrounds. And it's not what I'd call within driving distance, either. Wouldn't we be better off—''

''To stay right here and play sitting ducks? There isn't a courthouse in Minnesota that will be open again until Monday, and then there's a five-day waiting period. How certain are you that Jock wouldn't hear about his daughter applying for a marriage license in Minnesota—especially since it's the second one in just a few weeks?''

''You have a point,'' Kathryn admitted.

"We might as well spend the weekend on the road. We don't have to go all the way to Vegas, anyway, because anywhere inside the state line will do."

Kathryn sighed. "I suppose, if it's the best we can do, we should get started."

Back in the car, he thrust a road map at her and said, "Plot me a route to Wisconsin."

Kathryn stared at him. "Wisconsin? I wasn't the best geography student on the planet, but the last time I looked Wisconsin was due east of here, and Nevada is southwest. Why on earth do you want to go to Wisconsin?"

"To rob that bank you were talking about earlier." He flicked the turn signal and pulled onto the highway. He must have seen her expression, however, for he laughed. "Not literally, Katie. But we must get hold of some cash, so we're going to have to use the credit cards. If we use them along the way, we'll be giving Jock directions on how to follow us. So we'll go the opposite direction, create a false trail, then double back and make our run for Nevada."

She unfolded the map. "Don't tell me," she said as she buried her nose in it, trying to make out the fine print. "In your day job, you're a spy. Right?"

"Darn, you guessed my secret. Now the director will have to assassinate us both."

She put the map down. "You're excited about this," she accused. "You're enjoying it."

"Well…yeah, I suppose I am. Come on, Katie, this is an adventure we can tell our kids about."

Kathryn gulped.

He shot a look at her. "What's the matter? Hadn't you thought that far ahead yet?"

"I guess not," she admitted.

"Well, you'll have at least twenty-four hours to think it over before it's too late to change your mind," he said easily. "Probably more like thirty-six."

She turned back to the map, but she hardly saw it; the lines appeared to be squiggly.

Kids, she thought.

She and Douglas had never talked about the subject, but somehow she knew that they would have discussed having *children,* not *kids.* She'd never thought about the difference before, but suddenly it loomed as wide as the Gulf of Mexico. *Having children* with Douglas would have seemed almost clinical. *Having kids* with Jonah, on the other hand....

Would be one heck of a lot of fun, whispered a wicked little voice.

But she'd think about all that later. She ran a finger across the map. "This would have been easier if we'd started out in the right direction, you know."

"Well, if I'd realized when we left Duluth that we weren't headed for the Cities..." He sounded a bit absentminded.

"Okay. There's a place coming up where we can turn onto highway—"

But Jonah was obviously not listening. His gaze was fixed on the rearview mirror. "Damn," he said under his breath. "I didn't think even Jock could move this fast. But I'm not speeding, so—"

Kathryn twisted around to look. Behind them, precisely keeping pace, was a highway patrol car with the emergency lights running. And as she watched in disbelief, the siren began to wail, and the officer flashed his headlights, signaling them to pull off to the side of the road.

CHAPTER THREE

JONAH fumbled for his wallet and extracted his driver's license. "Don't say anything, Katie. Keep your head turned away—but not completely, because that looks suspicious."

She gave him an innocently wide-eyed look. "And I suppose you don't want me to make jokes about kidnappers, either?"

Jonah rolled down the window as the officer approached with his flashlight playing over the car.

"Good evening, sir," the officer said pleasantly. "Your driver's license and car registration, please." He took the documents, and his gaze slid easily from the photo on the license to Jonah's face and back. "Thank you, sir. I've been following you for a while. I presume you're not aware that your taillights are working only intermittently."

Taillights? This was only about taillights? Kathryn tried to choke back a gasp of relief.

"I certainly wasn't, Officer," Jonah said.

"I'll have to issue you a ticket for driving with defective equipment, of course. I'll be right back with the paperwork for you to sign."

"That was lucky," Kathryn breathed as he walked toward the cruiser.

"Don't get your hopes up too high."

"But if he stopped us because of the lights, then he couldn't have been looking specifically for us."

"Don't bet on it. Maybe he made up the bit about the lights as an excuse to check us out."

"How could he just make it up?"

"It's the 'working intermittently' part that makes me suspicious, because that's not easy to check. The lights could be working perfectly right now, but I can't exactly argue about something he says happened ten minutes ago and miles down the road."

The officer returned with a ticket pad in hand. "If you'll sign here, sir." He tore off the top layer and handed it to Jonah. "You realize, of course, that the law says the car cannot be driven further until the defect is fixed."

Jonah sounded calmer than Kathryn felt. "I suppose that means we'll have to get a tow truck out here. Since we are sitting on the edge of the highway—"

"You're actually in luck, sir. It could take an hour to get a tow truck out here."

"That's *lucky?*" Kathryn said under her breath.

"But the rules do allow me some discretion. Since you're only a couple of miles from a truck stop, my best judgment is that it would be better to let you drive that far than to leave you here on the side of the road for an hour or more to be a hazard to other traffic."

"I guess it *is* lucky," Kathryn muttered.

"If you'll proceed straight ahead to the first stop sign, the truck stop will be on your left at the junction with the main highway. They have some good mechanics in the garage there, and I think they usually have someone working on Sunday to handle emergencies. I'll follow you in, so you don't need to worry about traffic coming up behind you."

"That's very kind of you, Officer." Jonah's voice sounded a bit hollow.

He started the engine and waited till the officer was back in his patrol car. Then he pulled onto the highway and cautiously accelerated. The patrol car fell in behind them, emergency lights still running.

"A police escort into town," Kathryn said. "Just what we wanted. So now do you believe the lights aren't working right?"

"It doesn't matter much what I think, because that ticket says the wiring will have to be checked out by an approved mechanic before we can go anywhere. And that means we're stuck till at least tomorrow morning. Just keep your fingers crossed that we're the only emergency repair waiting when the garage opens."

Kathryn groaned, then brightened. "There's the stop sign. So that must be…" She looked across a complex of buildings, lit by a glare of high-powered street lamps. "The truck stop," she said faintly. "But where's the town?"

"Probably a few more miles down the road. Truck stops have a habit of locating where there are trucks— on the highways, outside the towns."

"Thank you very much for that lesson in economics, Mr. Clarke. I can't be seeing right—does that sign really say this place is called West Podunk?"

"Wouldn't surprise me. There's one in Iowa called Boondocks. This is actually a pretty big one. Restaurant, gas station, motel…"

"Jonah," she said with a tinge of panic. "The restaurant is a Katie Mae's."

"Honey, they're in every third town in the entire country. We were bound to run into one sooner or later.

That set of doors must be the garage.'' He took a parking spot outside and got out of the car, leaving the engine running.

The officer pulled alongside, called a cheerful good-bye, and was gone.

Kathryn scrambled out, as well, and joined Jonah at the back of the car. ''It's pretty dark back here,'' she pointed out.

''I noticed.'' Jonah jiggled the fender, and the tail-lights flickered on and back off as if on command. He shook his head. ''He's right, there's a short somewhere. Dammit, I'd have sworn this thing was in first-class condition.''

''And that's why you were under it this afternoon, I suppose. Because it's in such good shape.''

''I was changing the oil.''

Kathryn refrained from further comment, but only by biting her tongue. ''Now what do we do?''

''We pool our resources, go into the restaurant and order a meal, and hope that we can afford to check into the motel. Then we'll work on figuring out how we're going to pay the mechanic.'' Jonah shut off the engine and locked the car. ''I suppose things could be worse.''

''They certainly could. You could be in jail right now, and I could be looking for a lawyer to bail you out.''

''Taking things fifty-fifty,'' Jonah said with a note of approval. ''That's my girl. And if you couldn't find a lawyer, you could always use your nail file and break me out.''

They had enough cash to pay for their bacon and eggs, the biggest breakfast Kathryn had ever seen at any time of day. But it was apparent from a quick phone call to the motel that their resources would not stretch to cover a room.

"Then we'll sleep in the car," Kathryn said bravely, pushing her half-full plate away.

Jonah refilled his coffee cup. "Have you ever tried that? Not just dozing, I mean, but actually spending the night?"

"Well, no."

"Believe me, you'll be doing enough sleeping in the car on the way to Nevada. You don't want to start any sooner than you have to. I told them to hold the room."

"But if we can't pay for it—"

"The way things stand at the moment, we can't pay for the car repairs, either. We'll just have to hit the money machine for a cash advance."

"But that will leave a paper trail."

"I'd have preferred to wait till we were out of Minnesota, but we don't have a choice. Since I'm already in the official records as being here, we'll use my card tonight and keep yours clear till we get to Wisconsin."

"I thought maybe, with this happening, we'd just skip Wisconsin."

Jonah shook his head. "With this delay, it's even more important to lay a red herring for Jock to follow. But money isn't the only problem we've got right now. There's that ticket, too."

"Are you *still* being paranoid about that poor cop? He was only doing his job, Jonah."

"It's in the computer now. If your father thinks to ask for a driver's license check on me, that ticket will pop up—and he'll know where I am."

"Why would he do that? He probably doesn't have

any evidence that I'm with you," Kathryn objected. "You said yourself when the cop pulled us over that you didn't think Daddy could possibly have put the pieces together yet."

"It doesn't matter. Even if Jock isn't exactly suspicious of me, he's going to want his people to talk to everybody who was on the estate today, to find out what they might have seen. When I turn out to be hard to find, it would be only natural to ask the police to keep a lookout for my car. And if he would happen to do that before we manage to get the lights fixed—"

Kathryn winced. "We'll be saying 'Hello, Daddy' when his helicopter lands in the parking lot."

"And when he finds you here, Jock will be celebrating another stroke of his legendary good luck. To add to the problem, electrical systems can be tricky. Even a first-class mechanic might not be able to find the problem right away." He shook his head. "If we can't get out of town by noon tomorrow, we'll have to dump the car."

Kathryn's jaw dropped. "And do what instead? Take a bus? Or—wait, I've got it, a taxi! I'm sure there's a cab stand here somewhere, West Podunk has everything else."

"Don't be sarcastic, Katie Mae. Actually, the bus isn't a bad idea, except they take forever to get where you want to go. We'll buy another car."

"Using what? I don't know what kind of cash advances you can get on your credit card, but I don't generally buy cars with mine."

"I wasn't suggesting we get your Porsche now, just a serviceable set of wheels." He yawned. "Let's go draw out some cash and walk over to the motel to claim our room."

Our room. Since they could barely afford to check in at all, she could hardly demand her own quarters. And she'd look like a prude if she did, anyway, Kathryn told herself, considering that she was planning to marry the man as soon as it was humanly possible to do so.

She managed a smile. "Sure," she said. "I'm pretty tired myself."

She could hardly drag herself up the stairs to the second level and their room. Jonah threw open the door, and Kathryn hesitated just outside.

"Come on in, Katie," he said. "I'm not carrying you over the threshold till after the wedding."

She stepped past him. The room was small; two double beds had been squished into it, with barely enough space between them for a small nightstand. "Which bed do you want?"

"Doesn't matter much to me." Jonah closed the door behind her. "And you don't have to worry about sharing. I said you'd have at least twenty-four hours to make up your mind before you did anything that's irrevocable, and I'll stand by it."

Kathryn felt her eyelids begin to prickle. Of all the times to cry, she thought irritably. After everything she'd been through today, to get teary-eyed *now*... "Thanks," she whispered, and went to inspect the bathroom just so she could turn away before he suspected she was about to howl. "There's a bottle of shampoo, but no toothbrushes," she said over her shoulder. "And no robes, either."

"I thought you said you could do without luxuries."

She poked her head out. "Since when is a toothbrush a luxury?"

"A basket of scented goodies, Egyptian cotton towels,

and sparkling white terry-cloth bathrobes are. What did you expect for what we're paying, the Ritz?''

''I was just asking.''

''I'll go buy you a toothbrush while you have a shower. Anything else you need?''

''I can only think of a few dozen things.''

''Make a list and we'll get them tomorrow.'' He went out.

The water was both hot and abundant, and Kathryn stayed in it longer than she normally would have, allowing herself a good cry. Then she tried to wash away the traces of tears and wrapped herself in a towel. For the first time, she was beginning to realize the practical implications of having left home with only the clothes she was wearing.

And what an assortment of clothes, at that. Jeans, tailored shirt, and the wispiest, laciest white silk bra and panties she'd ever owned. Perfect to wear under her wedding gown, they were less than sensible for a woman on the run. But at least they'd dry fast. She squeezed a bit of shampoo into the sink so she could rinse out the lingerie.

She heard the squeak of a bedspring and a moment later Jonah, just outside the bathroom door, said, ''I hope you didn't use up all the hot water. I bought you a T-shirt. Want me to hand it in?''

Flooded with gratitude, she didn't stop to consider before she spoke. ''You know, I think I love you.''

''What?''

Her face flamed. ''I said thanks, Jonah, that was very thoughtful.'' She opened the door a crack and put out her hand.

The T-shirt was extra-large and bright purple, with a

picture of the West Podunk complex emblazoned across the front. When she came out of the bathroom, Jonah looked up from one of the beds, where he was sprawled with a road map spread out across the blanket. "I thought you'd make a real fashion statement wearing that, and I was right."

"And it'll be a souvenir, too. Plus it's long enough that I can wear it tomorrow as a dress. Not a bad buy at all." She sat down on the opposite side of the bed to look at his map. "What are you plotting now?"

"We need to get to Eau Claire before we use your credit card."

"All right, but why?"

"Because that's the first place we'll come to that's on the direct path between where we started and where we want Jock to think we're going."

"Which is…?"

"Either Milwaukee or Chicago—I thought it would be prudent to leave him some choice in the hope he'll get tangled up in it. We'll go on a spending spree with your card in Eau Claire and again in Madison. Then we'll put the card away and head straight southwest while—hopefully—Jock will keep searching toward the east."

Kathryn studied the map, adding mileage counts in her head. "If we have to wait awhile for the car, we probably aren't going to get to Eau Claire till late afternoon."

"That's about right."

"Well, isn't it going to look like it's taken us an awfully long time to travel just a hundred and fifty miles?"

Jonah sounded absentminded. "That's an easy one.

As soon as your father realizes you aren't alone, he won't have any trouble at all figuring out what happened.''

''He won't?''

''Nope. It's because we stopped a few times along the way so I could ravish you.''

Kathryn caught her breath and had to force herself to relax. It took effort to keep her voice light. ''In that case, it's no wonder I'm so tired.''

He looked up from the map, and his smile made her heart turn over in her chest.

Jonah was already waiting outside the garage when the mechanic arrived to open up. The man surveyed him sympathetically, agreed to check out the taillights first thing, and sent him off as if, Jonah thought, he was a six-year-old being sent out to play for a couple of hours.

He stopped in the gas station to buy a Sunday newspaper and debated whether to go back up to the motel room or into the restaurant.

The restaurant was without a doubt the safer choice. Kathryn had still been asleep when he'd left the room half an hour before; she'd been curled on her side under a sheet that had been washed so many times it was almost sheer, with one hand flung out in what looked like an invitation. It was a picture he wasn't likely to forget anytime soon.

The fact was, if she was still in bed when he went back, he'd have all he could do not to climb in with her and say to hell with gentlemanly guarantees. If he'd had any idea when he'd made that promise what his Katie Mae looked like in nothing but a T-shirt, with her black hair spread over a stark white pillow, he'd have thought twice about opening his mouth and issuing foolish pledges.

And even if she was already dressed when he went back, he'd taken a good look while he shaved at the wispy bits of lingerie hanging on the towel rack. Now every time he looked at her he'd be picturing what lay underneath....

Definitely the restaurant would be a safer choice. But he turned toward the motel room anyway.

And stopped beside the pay phone, fumbling for change in his pocket. There was a call he needed to make, and he couldn't put it off any longer.

He'd left his disposable razor lying beside the sink, but at least he'd washed away all the evidence of using it. Whatever else the man was—gentle, kind, sometimes cynical and usually a bit suspicious—he wasn't a slob.

Kathryn gathered the razor up along with their few other possessions—the road maps, the tube of toothpaste, her West Podunk T-shirt—and packed them in the red plastic bag he'd brought from the little shop the night before.

She had to admit it was the quickest and easiest packing-up she'd ever done. Compared to the way she'd agonized over exactly what to take to Bermuda, this trip was a honeymoon.

The thought brought her up short. *That's exactly what it is.*

It was a topsy-turvy kind of honeymoon where the trip came before the wedding. A backwards honeymoon—but a honeymoon nevertheless.

She was still thinking about that, and wondering if Jonah would laugh at the idea or be taken aback by it, when she reached the bottom of the motel stairs. She paused to look around, debating whether to check the garage first or the restaurant.

She wasn't expecting to see him immediately, and at first her brain refused to believe what she was looking at. In fact, Jonah was in the last place she'd have thought to look for him—not far from the gas station pumps, leaning into the pay phone kiosk with his back to her. She could barely make out the telephone, cradled between his jaw and his shoulder.

Kathryn was stunned.

She gritted her teeth and marched over to confront him. As if he'd felt her coming closer, he hung up the phone and turned to face her when she was less than six feet away. "Breakfast first," he asked easily, "or shall we hit the shop and buy the rest of our necessities while we wait for the car?"

Was Jonah really as much at ease as he appeared? There was something different in his expression, she thought. Regret? Concern because of what she might have overheard?

"Neither," she said firmly. "I'd like to know who you were calling."

"A friend."

"Oh, really? The woman you stood up for a date last night, maybe?"

A smile tugged at the corner of his mouth. "Careful, Katie," he murmured, "or somebody might think you're jealous."

Kathryn wanted to kick him. How dare he accuse her of acting jealous? She wasn't the one making phone calls behind her partner's back. He had some nerve, talking about sharing equally in everything and then doing this.

"As a matter of fact," Jonah went on, "his name's Brian, he's a supervisor at the company I work for, and I just left him a message that I won't be coming in tomorrow."

Kathryn felt a bit deflated. "I guess I'd forgotten about that. Your job, I mean."

"I noticed. Not all of us can take time off without an excuse."

She bristled. "I do work, you know. I arranged months ago to have this week off."

"And if you had let me know a little earlier that we were going to take this road trip," he said mildly, "I'd have planned farther ahead, too."

Kathryn bit her lip. "I'm sorry, Jonah."

"It's all right, Katie Mae." He flicked a finger against her cheek.

The fleeting contact left her feeling more alone than ever. "Don't call me that," she protested automatically. "Not when we're standing right outside one of the restaurants. What are you going to do about the rest of the week?"

"Call in every day, I suppose. Don't worry, I doubt very much that Brian's phone has a trace on it."

"Jonah...what if you lose your job over this stunt?"

"Then I guess I'll have to rely on your promise to give me fifteen percent of Katie Mae's Kitchens." His voice softened. "You thought I was calling Jock, didn't you?"

She nodded.

"Why would I do that, Katie?"

"I don't know. Maybe because you're tired of being saddled with me, but you didn't want to tell me that." She bit her lip.

"So I call your father, he swoops in and does the bad-guy imitation, and I'm still the hero? I'll keep that plan in mind in case I do get tired of you. In the meantime...come here."

She didn't intend to obey, but she must have stepped forward, because suddenly his arm was around her shoulders and he was drawing her close.

Her body fit perfectly against his, and automatically—as if she'd done it a thousand times—she tipped her head back to the precise angle where his mouth could most easily find hers. His lips were warm and firm against hers—first simply nibbling, then growing more certain with each touch, demanding her response, until her mind was swimming and her surroundings began to look like the view from an out-of-control carousel.

By the time Jonah raised his head, she was breathless and everything around her had turned slightly blue. Not that she cared. Though she was incapable of speech, she raised a hand to his neck to pull him down to her once more.

"Breakfast," Jonah said sternly. "Or the idea of being ravished won't be a joke anymore."

A chorus of whistles and cheers from a group of truckers who had lined up at the gasoline pumps to watch brought Kathryn back to earth with a bang. She felt color flood over her, and she ducked her head against Jonah's shoulder and let him lead her into the restaurant.

She'd been too worried and worn out last night to pay much attention to her surroundings, other than being careful not to get too close to the photos of a dark-haired child which featured in the decor of every Katie Mae's Kitchen. Surely nobody would note a resemblance—and even if someone did, there must be hundreds of women of all ages who looked rather like the child she had once been. But it was only sensible to be careful.

This morning, however, her regular instincts had kicked in, and as the hostess led them to a table, Kathryn noted details. Napkins, flatware, table decorations. Was that just a shadow, or was there dust on the ledge above a booth?

"Let me guess," Jonah said as the hostess went out of hearing range. "You're the one who sets the standards for the whole franchise."

"Is it that obvious?"

"Only to someone who knows your secret. To the average person you'd just appear to be very observant and terribly choosy."

"Thanks. Observant and choosy—that's my job description in a nutshell."

"No wonder you were jittery at the idea of coming in here. If you go 'round visiting the restaurants—"

"Not often. I'm really just a small cog in the gears at the corporate office." She closed the menu and laid it aside—upside down, so the picture on the front wasn't visible. "I think I'll just have a muffin and coffee. I assume you brought that newspaper in to read?"

Jonah passed it across to her. "Don't be shocked if you come face to face with your photograph."

"Oh, no, I hadn't even thought of that possibility."

"A bride vanishes—apparently into thin air—just a few minutes before her wedding. Sounds like news to me."

She turned the pages with caution, and only crumbs were left of her muffin before she finished reading. But finally she sat back from the last section with a sigh of relief. "Nothing."

"Give your father time. You hadn't been gone very long when the presses rolled last night." He leveled a long, assessing look at her. "You need to cut your hair."

"And you need to jump in the lake," Kathryn said pleasantly.

"It would be a shame, I agree, but it would eliminate a whole lot of Katie sightings if you changed your hairstyle."

"Oh, that's what you meant. I thought you were making a general comment about my grooming." She tore a corner off the sports section.

"Wait just a minute, I haven't read that."

"You told me to make a list of the things we needed to buy."

"Yes, but you could use something less important than sports to write it on."

She ignored him. "We're going to need more clothes, of course."

"That'll have to wait till we get out of here. The selection in the gift shop is pretty limited. By the way, I thought you were going to wear your West Podunk T-shirt as a dress today."

"I thought better of it," Kathryn said dryly. "I figured a whole lot of people would want one and ask where I got it. It would just draw too much attention. So what are we going to do for clothes?"

"We'll keep an eye out for a secondhand shop."

"Good. I've never been in one—can you imagine what Daddy would say?—but one of the girls at work has an Armani suit that she bought for less than half of what it cost new."

"Katie," he said gently. "That's not the kind of secondhand shop I mean."

"Oh. Well, I'm sure you'll find a good one. I need hand lotion and nail polish remover—would you believe I had a manicure on Friday and I've already chipped a nail?"

He glanced at the bill. "No wonder your father's a multimillionaire. At that price, your muffin should have been studded with gold nuggets instead of raisins. Let's see if the gift shop has some kind of cooler that we can fill with ice so we can take cheese and cold cuts and stuff like that with us."

"Picnic our way across the country?"

"It'll save us time and money. Oh, and we'll want a roll of duct tape."

"What for?"

"I don't know right now. But you can fix darned near anything with duct tape. I once—" He glanced out the window and did a double take.

"What are you looking at?" Kathryn said frantically.

"I think I just found us a set of wheels."

She closed her eyes for an instant in relief. "Is that all? The way you looked, I thought my father and the entire Seventh Cavalry were riding in."

"Hey, this is a pretty big deal, considering there's no car dealer out here in Podunk. Finding something that's not only for sale but is in our price range isn't an easy thing."

"How do you know it's in our price range?" She studied the cars outside. "Where?"

He reached across the table, took hold of her chin, and turned her face till she was looking at the very edge of the parking lot. "The one with the For Sale sign in the window," he said gently.

Kathryn didn't believe her eyes. "*No.* I am not going

to Nevada in that…vehicle. Let me rephrase that. I am not going *anywhere* in that vehicle.''

"That's exactly what I thought you'd say. And that's why it's perfect. If a hundred different people would call up Jock Campbell personally to tell him they'd seen his daughter riding across the country in what you call *that vehicle,* he wouldn't believe a one of them.''

She looked out the window again, noting faded blue paint, a dented fender, and a pair of fuzzy pink dice dangling from the mirror of an old pickup truck. A truck with a For Sale sign in the window.

No wonder Jonah was certain they could afford it. If the current owner had any sense at all, he'd pay them to take it off his hands.

She sighed and picked up her pen. "That reminds me of a couple of other things we're going to need,'' she said. "Aspirin and antacids. Personally, I think we should buy the giant economy size.''

CHAPTER FOUR

THE truck's cab smelled musty, and though Kathryn had tied a pine-scented air freshener to the fuzzy pink dice hanging from the rearview mirror, Jonah wouldn't bet any money on when it might actually make a difference in the atmosphere. The inside handle on the passenger door was missing, so a rider could only get out by lowering the window and reaching for the outside latch. He was just glad Kathryn hadn't noticed the bumper stickers yet. He didn't think she'd see the humor in driving across the country displaying sentiments like *Honk If You Love Harleys* and *Possum Hunters Do It In The Spotlight.*

And of course, the gas tank was almost empty. "It's axiomatic," Jonah said. "When you buy a used vehicle, it never has any gas in it. But I'm sure you wouldn't know that firsthand, Katie."

"Used? Don't you mean 'used up'? We're lucky this thing still has a steering wheel." She gave the cooler a push.

He'd miscalculated the size of the cab, and the insulated cooler he'd picked out barely fit on the floor of the front seat. He kept one eye on the gas pump and the other on Kathryn as she tried out various positions—feet atop the cooler, folded under her on the seat, or stretched at an unnatural angle toward the center of the cab.

"At least my purchase fits *under* the seat," she grumbled, finally propping her feet on the dashboard.

"Your purchase," he said, "shouldn't be allowed to fit anywhere."

"You'd better not throw it out!"

"I won't. I'll put it in the back of the truck and hope someone steals it. They might, if it's wrapped so they can't see what they're getting."

"You're just aggravated because I spent your money on it."

"It was our money, and I'm aggravated because we need to be getting value for every penny, not buying trash."

"I've already said I'll pay you back when we get to Eau Claire."

"You're missing the point, Katie. We're going to need every cent we can get from your credit card. Spending our cash on junky plaster trinkets—"

"It's not junk," she said indignantly, "it's not plaster, and it's not a trinket."

"A fifteen-inch-long scale model of the West Podunk truck stop is not what I'd call a work of art."

"I didn't say it was. It's a souvenir. I may never get back here again."

"Oh, no? We'd better be coming back, since I'm leaving my car. Speaking of which…I wonder where the mechanic went with my credit card."

"I still don't see why you gave it to him."

"Because when the repair work is done, he'll want to be paid. If he has the credit card number, he can run the charge through as soon as he's finished."

"Obviously. But by that time your card may have been flagged."

"That's the beauty of it, because when the transaction comes through, it'll look like I'm still here. Meanwhile, you'll have been hitting cash machines in Wisconsin and it will appear that you're headed due east. If Jock has added things up by then and figured out that we're together, that should confuse him all over again.''

"It certainly confuses *me*," Kathryn muttered.

The mechanic appeared from around the corner of the gas pump and handed Jonah the credit card. His gaze, however, was fixed on Kathryn. "Buddy," he said softly, "if I was stranded in West Podunk with a woman like her, the last thing on my mind would be getting my taillights fixed. What you've got here is a whole lot better than the average guy's excuse for getting stuck in the middle of nowhere with a pretty girl. But you aren't even taking advantage of it, man. You should have your head examined, buying this piece of junk and driving off in it."

Jonah let his voice drop into a confidential tone. "We're having a little problem staying ahead of her father."

The mechanic nodded wisely. "Trying to arrange a shotgun wedding, is he? Well, I'd say there'd be worse things than letting him catch you. But hey—anybody comes through asking about you, I haven't seen a thing."

"Thanks. And take good care of my car, will you? I'll be back for it as soon as I can."

"When the dust settles, right? Sure, I'll look after it personally. As soon as it's repaired, I'll park it way in the back of the garage where nobody ever looks." The mechanic walked off across the parking lot, whistling.

Jonah paid for the gas and slid behind the wheel. "I think we're ready to roll, Katie."

"Speak for yourself," she muttered. "If I work hard

at it, I might be prepared by next year sometime. What
were you and the mechanic talking about?''

"You. He thinks I'm an idiot to leave West Podunk
when I could be snuggled up in a motel room with you."

She made a disparaging noise. "You're sure he wasn't
lecturing you about what an idiot you were to buy this
truck?"

"Of course not. The engine's in great shape. It'll get
us to Nevada and back, wait and see."

"It won't have to get me back. Once we're married,
it doesn't matter if Daddy finds us, right?—because all
he can do then is sputter about it. So I'll be able to use
my credit card wherever I want—and I'm flying first
class. It's up to you whether you come along or drive
the clunker all the way back."

"Wait and see, Katie. You might be downright fond
of this clunker by the time we get to Nevada."

Kathryn looked as if she thought pigs would fly before
that happened. But she didn't bother to answer, just gave
a sigh of resignation and fastened her seat belt.

The sky began to darken just as they started around the
Twin Cities, but the truck's engine was noisy enough
that it took a while for Kathryn to realize she was hearing thunder, too. By the time they reached the Wisconsin
border, rain was coming down in dark gray sheets,
blowing across the highway in gusts that sometimes
meant they couldn't even see the lights of the enormous
recreational vehicle in front of them. Traffic slowed to
a crawl. The wipers could scarcely keep up, and when
the road turned to angle into the storm, cold rain blasted
through a gap at the top of the passenger door and spat-
tered across Kathryn's face and neck.

She shrieked, and Jonah slammed on the brakes. "What the—"

"I'm getting wet!"

"Is that all? You sounded as if we were about to hit something. The gasket on that door must be worn out."

"What a surprise. Paper towels—why didn't I think to buy a roll of paper towels?"

"Because you were too busy picking out your architectural marvel."

"Leave my souvenir out of this. You didn't think of paper towels, either. I don't suppose we could use your duct tape to seal up the gap in the door?"

"It wouldn't stick very well on wet metal."

"Figures." She wiped at her face with a tissue, which promptly disintegrated. "This is not only wet, it's cold."

"Rain usually is. Here, slide across into the middle of the seat. You'll be more comfortable where you can stretch your legs out, anyway."

"More comfortable than what?" Kathryn muttered. "If the choice is between this truck and the wing chair in my bedroom…"

Jonah didn't look at her. "We're not far from Eau Claire now. All you have to do is call Jock collect and he'll send out the rescue squad."

"You know that's not what I meant, Jonah."

"Really? It sounds to me like you're having second thoughts about this scheme."

"Why on earth would I be feeling disillusioned? Heavens, at the current rate of progress it appears we'll be in Nevada by Christmas." She slid across the seat toward him and fumbled to fasten the middle seat belt. The belt was short and the latch was next to Jonah's thigh, and one thing was immediately apparent to

Kathryn—she didn't need to worry about being cold anymore. She was practically pressed against his side; he could probably feel her heart pounding.

"Traveling slowly isn't a bad idea," Jonah mused. "Jock sure won't be looking for you this close to home." He glanced down at her and said gently, "Are you certain you're not having regrets, Katie Mae?"

"Why? Are you?"

"Nope. Once I make up my mind to do something, I do it. But I thought perhaps you were starting to miss what's-his-name."

"Douglas? No."

"It's nothing to be ashamed of, you know—missing him. You intended to marry the man, after all. Even finding out his nasty little secret couldn't have wiped out all the feelings you had for him."

Half surprised that she hadn't thought of it herself, Kathryn probed cautiously around the corners of her mind, looking for regrets. But she couldn't find any. Not where Douglas was concerned, at any rate. She did feel a twinge of sadness that she'd embarrassed her father in front of all his guests, but not where her ex-fiancé was concerned. There was anger, of course, and indignation over how he had treated her. But there was no regret that things hadn't worked out differently.

I must be incredibly shallow, she thought. Not much better than Douglas himself, in fact. It was probably just as well she was planning a hasty, cold bargain of a marriage, for it wouldn't be fair to a man who did care about her—if there was such a creature—to marry him if she couldn't feel the same way he did. *It was pure good luck that I ran across Jonah,* she thought.

"I'm just in a funk," she said. "Ignore me."

"That's the one thing no man could do, Katie."

Startled by the almost-somber note in his voice, Kathryn turned to stare up at him. It was only midafternoon, but the storm made it look like twilight, and with his gaze fixed on the road, she couldn't clearly read his expression.

He glanced at her and grinned almost ruefully. "I guess I'm in a funk, too. I'll ignore yours if you'll ignore mine."

"Deal."

He reached for her hand and placed it palm down on his thigh, cupping his own over it. The warmth of him sank deep into her fingers and seemed to radiate out, sending relaxation though her muscles, and when after a couple of minutes he put his hand back on the steering wheel she felt as if he'd set her adrift. It took her a moment to realize that she was still leaning against him, with her palm still resting in a position that—while not exactly intimate—was certainly more familiar than any she'd ever taken with Douglas. She yanked her hand away and leaned forward to fiddle with the buttons on the radio.

"Trying to get a weather report?" There was a dry note in Jonah's voice.

"We'd feel pretty foolish if we half drowned trying to get from the truck to a cash machine, and then ten minutes later the rain stopped."

"It's not likely to dry up anytime soon. That's Eau Claire up ahead."

"Good. I'll start watching for a bank. There should be something along the highway."

"I'd rather drive a ways into town. That way it won't look like we're passing through in a hurry."

She sat back and eyed him thoughtfully. "Does your busy little mind ever stop generating intrigues, Jonah?"

"No. But it isn't often I have this much material to work with."

"You should set up a business. Sort of like a cross between a private investigator and a tailor—Schemes and Scams, made to order to fit the customer. How far into town do you think we'll have to go?"

"You're anxious to get this over with, aren't you?"

She nodded. "I'll feel better when we've got some money again. You're right, I shouldn't have spent all that cash on a silly souvenir."

He ruffled her hair. "It'll be all right, Katie Mae."

She wanted to lean against him again in order to truly soak up the comfort she felt in his touch and heard in his slightly gruff voice.

"If we run low," Jonah went on, "I'll just put you to work scrubbing floors somewhere until you earn it back."

Not only did Kathryn's credit card perform like a trouper when—holding her breath—she pushed it into a cash machine in downtown Eau Claire, but on the way out of town they drove by a Salvation Army resale store. "It wasn't exactly Armani," Kathryn said as they stashed two bags behind the seat of the truck. "And I don't think brown paper grocery bags are going to catch on as luggage, especially in rainy climates. But I really like my new sweater and that pair of cargo pants you bought." She climbed into the cab. "I suppose now it's on to Madison?"

Jonah drummed his fingertips on the steering wheel. "Partway, at least. We probably shouldn't stay in Eau

Claire. But I'm thinking, because that withdrawal went so smoothly, that it might be worth trying to make a really big score in Madison.''

"Like what?" she said warily.

"Take the card into a bank. You should be able to get a much bigger cash advance in person than from a machine.''

"But banks aren't open on Sunday nights.''

"So we stay overnight and hit the bank first thing tomorrow. To tell the truth, the way that rain keeps coming down, I wouldn't mind being off the highway anyway, especially when it starts getting really dark. Look at the map and see where we might find a little motel between here and Madison.''

"If we're going to have plenty of money,'' Kathryn said wistfully, "maybe we could go on into the city and stay someplace really nice.''

Jonah shook his head. "Even if you're paying cash, major hotels won't let you check in without showing a credit card. And they run it through first thing to make sure it's good, before you get a room key.''

"But Daddy hasn't put a hold on my card, or I couldn't have gotten the money.''

"A hold would stop you from using it at all. I'm betting he hasn't done anything that would prevent you from charging your way clear across the country. He's probably just got a flag on the account, so as soon as a charge is posted the credit card company calls him to tell him where it came from. And if he got a call saying that you'd used the card to check into some fancy hotel in Madison, Wisconsin, he'd have a good ten hours to catch up with us. No, we're limited to mom-and-pop operations that understand cash.''

Kathryn sighed. "Why do you always have to be so logical? And so right?" She spread out the map and squinted at it in the stormy half light, then pointed. "That-a-way, oh, trusty chauffeur."

"That reminds me. You told me yesterday that you make pretty good time on the highway yourself."

"If this is a roundabout way of asking me to drive, no thanks."

"You wouldn't have to turn yourself into a pretzel to fit around the cooler, if you were driving."

"But you would, and I'd probably never hear the last of it. So I think I'll still refuse the honor."

"We agreed to split things fifty-fifty, Katie Mae."

"Tell you what," she said brightly. "I'll give up my half ownership in this truck if you don't make me get behind the wheel."

"If I'm doing all the driving it'll take even longer to get to Nevada," he warned.

"So instead of Christmas, maybe we'll get there by Valentine's Day? What the heck, February in the desert has to be warmer than it is in Minnesota."

"You mean you don't go to Arizona or the Caribbean every winter?"

"For a couple of weeks, maybe. But obviously you don't work for my father or you wouldn't even ask." She yawned. "As long as I'm back to work by next Monday…"

They drove for another hour, but when the rain kept on and the lines on the highway almost disappeared because the surface was so dark and wet, Jonah called a halt and pulled into the next motel. When he came back out of the office, however, he was wearing a frown and he wasn't carrying a key. "Everybody's pulling in off the road because of the weather," he said. "And just to add spice to the mix, there's an antique show setting up in Madison for the week, so dealers are coming in from all directions. The clerk called another motel down the road a few miles, and they're saving a room for us. But it appears to be the only one available for fifty miles in any direction."

"It must have been a female clerk," Kathryn muttered. "Going to that much trouble for you."

Jonah protested, "I didn't do her any damage—"

"—In the course of getting what you wanted. I know, I know. You're probably right, she'll just dream of your smile for the next three weeks."

They almost missed the motel, which was set far back from the highway. And as soon as they reached the room, Kathryn realized that the note of warning in Jonah's voice had been there with good reason. Not only was the room even smaller than the one they'd had at West Podunk, but the drapes were hanging askew, the night table was marred with cigarette burns, and there was only one bed.

She decided not to look too closely at her surroundings. "The only room for fifty miles, I believe you said? I guess that means we make the best of it."

"I'll sleep on the floor."

She glanced at the dingy carpet and grimaced. "Don't be silly. We'll share."

His eyes brightened. "Katie, sweetheart—"

"The chauffeur must have his rest." She looked straight at him. "And believe me, I mean *rest*."

"The twenty-four hours I promised you are up," Jonah reminded.

"And we're a whole lot farther from Nevada than we were when you made that promise."

"If that means you intend to wait till the wedding—"

"That's exactly what I mean." When he yawned, she added dryly, "And a very good idea it is, too."

"Just goes to show how much you don't know about men. But since you've obviously made up your mind, how about a pizza? We passed a delivery place back a ways."

"You're the accountant. Can we afford it?"

"The chauffeur must have his nourishment, too, and I'm not going out in that rain again—just listen to it. Besides, we'll be in the money tomorrow, after we hit the bank."

"Don't make it sound like we're planning to rob it. The way this motel is built, people three rooms down could be listening to us talk."

Jonah grinned. "I see—it's not the prospect of the wedding that's holding you back, it's the thought of being overheard. Well, that makes me feel much better." He picked up the telephone. "How do you like your pizza? Mushrooms? Pepperoni? Green pepper?"

"I don't care, as long as it doesn't have anchovies."

His eyes narrowed. "That must mean Douglas was an anchovy man."

"You can't pick them off, either. I mean, you *can*— but it doesn't do any good, because the taste sinks right into the crust." She wrinkled her nose.

"And you were still going to marry this guy?" Jonah shook his head. "Katie...oh, Katie."

"Well, I wasn't going to make lifetime decisions based on pizza," she said, annoyed. "If he'd taken me to a pizza place a second time, I'd have ordered my own.''

''Exactly how long did you date this guy?''

''Two years, more or less. Why?''

''He bought you one pizza, in two years? I don't suppose he liked burritos, either, or dim sum.''

''The only ethnic food he seemed to be interested in was French,'' Kathryn admitted.

''Hmm. In that case, I suppose I should warn you that I refuse to eat at a restaurant whose name I can't pronounce. Other than that, anything goes.''

''I'll keep that in mind,'' Kathryn murmured.

She unpacked their plastic bag full of toiletries while he was on the phone. It felt odd to set two toothbrushes upright in a plastic drinking glass, rather than just one… But that was how it was going to be from now on. If she actually went through with this. If she actually married him.

Earlier, Jonah had asked if she was having second thoughts, and she'd denied it. But maybe it was time for second thoughts, and third ones, too. She'd been leaping from one decision to the next ever since she'd walked out on her balcony yesterday and listened as the usher turned her world upside down…

But the decision to run had been a good one, there was no question about that. If she had needed confirmation that the usher's story was truth, she'd gotten it in that brief conversation with her father last night. *Douglas is here,* Jock had told her. *He's willing to let bygones be bygones…* She frowned as she thought it over.

''Jonah,'' she called.

''Yeah?'' He turned off the television set.

She leaned against the doorjamb and surveyed him. "If you were engaged to a woman…"

"I *am* engaged," he reminded. "To you. Remember?"

"Yes, but if you were engaged to someone else, and she—"

"Katie Mae, is this is one of those hypothetical questions women love so much? Because I feel a bad case of hives coming on."

She fixed him with a glare.

He winced. "All right, go ahead."

"If the woman you were engaged to walked out on the wedding, would you still want to marry her?"

"Is this a trick question? It depends on why she did it."

"Aha. Of course. That's exactly what I thought—you'd want an explanation. And I don't doubt that you'd be a bear till you got it, too."

"Yes, I probably would." Jonah sounded cautious. "Now do you want to explain why we're having this conversation?"

"Last night Daddy told me that Douglas still wanted to marry me."

"I guess I don't see why that surprises you."

"It doesn't. But it confirms that the usher was right."

"Wait a minute. What usher?"

"The one I overheard talking about Douglas's gambling debts. If he'd been wrong—if Douglas wasn't up to his ears in financial trouble—he would have wanted an explanation of why I didn't show up for the wedding. But he didn't ask, which means he already knew. He just said, 'We've both made mistakes.' Which means he was admitting—"

"Hold it, Katie. You walked out on the man because of something you *overheard?*"

"Yes," she said slowly. "But I was right, so what difference does it make?"

Jonah shook his head as if to clear it. "This has never exactly sounded like a match made in heaven, but—"

Kathryn wasn't listening anymore. She had all the confirmation she needed. The decision she had made on an instant's consideration—to run away rather than go through with the wedding—had been a better choice than the one she'd considered for two years—to marry Douglas. Maybe she was just better at spur-of-the-moment decisions than reasoned-out ones...

A knock at the door startled her. Jonah negotiated with the delivery person and set the pizza at the end of the bed. Kathryn folded herself up cross-legged beside it and dug in.

Jonah lounged on the other side of the pizza. "You should call your father again."

"And get another lecture about why I should come straight home and how faithful, broken-hearted Douglas is waiting for me?" Kathryn shook her head. "Don't even think about it. Aren't you eating? This is wonderful."

He shrugged and reached for a slice. "I'll flip you for who gets the shower first."

"Go ahead. It's your turn."

She cleaned up the pizza debris, then sat by the window and watched it rain until he came out of the bathroom. She took her time with her own shower, then brushed her hair a hundred strokes and rubbed lotion into every inch of skin. By the time she was finished, Jonah was asleep and breathing deeply—just as she'd hoped he would be.

Or had she? Was that the tiniest curl of disappointment in the pit of her stomach?

She slid carefully under the blanket and stretched out, trying to find a comfortable position. Lying on her right side, facing him, she found she couldn't keep her eyes closed. The dim glow from the streetlight outside let her see only the outlines of his face and the slow rise and fall of his bare chest where the blanket had slipped down, but that was enough to make her nervous. When she shifted to her left side, with her back to him, she found herself clinging to the edge of the mattress to keep from sliding toward the middle of the bed. Did the mattress really sag in the center, she wondered, or was she feeling a little dizzy because of the situation—and her own uncertainty about it?

Kathryn woke to the soothing touch of a warm hand stroking her back—the way her mother had always awakened her. She stretched in utter relaxation and opened her eyes to find herself nose to nose with Jonah. And she was looking down at him.

It took her a moment to figure out what had happened. The sagging mattress had not been a figment of her imagination; there really was a concave spot in the center, and during the night he'd slipped down into the hollow. Then somehow she'd rolled over on top of him, and here they were, with the length of their bodies pressed together, warm and intimate and knowing. His hand was still stroking her back, but now he seemed to be trying to melt her muscles into his....

"Hi," he said softly. "I've been lying here thinking

about things. I know I promised not to ravish you, but I don't think I said anything at all about whether you could ravish me. And I've decided that I don't object at all. In fact, I'll be happy to cooperate in any—''

Kathryn braced both hands against his chest and pushed herself up and away.

"Ouch," he complained. "That's not very nice, you know, using me like a handrail, when I was acting like a perfect gentleman."

She fixed him with a look.

"Well, almost," he admitted with a grin. "But you have to admit you're a spoilsport, Katie." With some difficulty he levered himself out of the bed.

Kathryn sat on the edge and pretended not to watch as he prowled across the room and pulled back the drapes to look outside.

It would have been terrifyingly easy to give in to the warm pressure of his hand, to turn her face just an inch until his lips met hers, to let him make love to her.

So why hadn't she? she asked herself.

And why—now that it was too late—was she wishing she had?

Jonah had the truck's hood raised and was underneath it, examining the engine, when Kathryn brought the last of their belongings out of the motel room. He stole a sideways look at her as she approached, concluding that his Katie wasn't displaying quite as much cool self-control this morning as she'd like to think she was. He started to whistle.

She paused beside the passenger door of the truck. "What's this?"

"It was a good idea you had, to tape around the door so it couldn't rain in."

She glanced at the sky. "There isn't a cloud in sight."

"Never know what we'll run into by nightfall."

"The truth is, you just don't want to have to walk around the truck to open my door every time we stop."

"I do seem to be having to use up all my gentlemanly instincts in other directions today," he mused, and smothered a grin as she turned pink.

She walked around the truck and put her paper bag behind the seat. "Where did you put the duct tape?"

"In the tool box. Why?"

"Because I want to use it."

He finished pouring oil into the engine, wiped his hands, and lowered the hood with a bang. Walking around the truck, he saw that *Honk If You Love Harleys* had already vanished under a strip of shiny gray tape and she was measuring out another length to cover *Possum Hunters Do It In The Spotlight*.

"You're right," Kathryn said with satisfaction, handing him the roll of tape. "You *can* fix darned near anything with this stuff."

Delighted, he brushed a kiss across the top of her head. "Katie Mae, you make a great moll. Remind me to bring you along every time I plan to knock off a bank."

She sniffed and climbed into the cab. "Come on, let's get this over with."

They were still half an hour from Madison, and by the time they reached the city they'd rehearsed the moves. Even so, Jonah was feeling tense by the time Kathryn reached the teller window, handed over her credit card, and said, "I'd like to get the maximum cash advance that the card allows."

The teller sounded bored. "I'll need a photo identification." She zipped the credit card through a slot on her computer keyboard.

Kathryn held up her driver's license. Still looking at the screen, the teller stretched out a hand and took it. But before she even looked at the laminated identification card, the teller paused and frowned. Her gaze flicked across Kathryn and appeared to linger on Jonah. "Excuse me," she said. "I seem to be having a problem with my computer. I'll have to process this at another station. I'll be right back with your card and ID."

The teller didn't wait for an answer. With Kathryn's credit card and driver's license in her hand, she hurried out of sight.

CHAPTER FIVE

KATHRYN was too shocked to move. Jonah reached past her as if to toy with a paperclip which was lying at the teller's station; the movement brought his lips close to her ear, and he whispered, "Walk toward the door as if your business is finished. And take it slowly. Don't look as if you're in a hurry."

"But I have to wait for my credit card," Kathryn protested automatically. "To say nothing of my driver's license. She said she'd be right back."

Her heart began to thud even harder as she realized that Jonah looked as if he expected a SWAT team to swoop down on them any moment.

Seeing alarm in his eyes sent Kathryn to the edge of panic. "Whatever you say," she gulped.

Strolling across the bank lobby as if she didn't have a care in the world was one of the more difficult things Kathryn had ever done, and she didn't manage a full breath until they were outside and almost to the truck, parked nearly half a block from the bank's front door.

She slid in through the driver's door and under the steering wheel to her now-habitual spot in the middle. "Now I see why you chose such an out-of-the-way corner of the lot," she muttered. "But if you really thought we might have security guards after us—"

Jonah shook his head. "I didn't. It's just that parking in the far corners means there's less chance of getting a

78

dent from another car." He started the engine and eased out onto the street.

Kathryn glanced back; the parking lot appeared perfectly normal and it seemed no one was even looking their way. Suddenly, she was half giddy with relief. "You were worried about getting a dent in this thing? How would you even know if someone hit it?"

"It's become a habit to be careful where I park, no matter what I'm driving." He sounded absentminded.

She glanced at the speedometer. "Can we hurry a little, Jonah? I know it looks at the moment as if no one is following us, but just to be on the safe side—"

"No. We'd only draw attention to ourselves."

"Like the truck itself isn't memorable enough?"

"With any luck, no one at the bank even saw it. The teller went toward the back, the side of the building away from the parking lot, and we were out of there before anyone else had a reason to be suspicious or watchful."

Kathryn sighed. "Leaving my credit card behind. *And* my driver's license."

"Losing your license is a nuisance, no question about it. But it doesn't matter much where the credit card ends up, because it's worthless from here on out."

"Now that Daddy's reported it as stolen." Her voice was flat.

"At first," Jonah said thoughtfully, "that's what I figured he'd done, too. But that isn't necessarily what triggered the teller's caution. I don't think the status of the account has changed at all since we made that withdrawal last night. It's more likely the teller just overreacted to whatever warning popped up when she plugged the number in."

Kathryn shook her head. "She was acting as if that card was as hot as a truckload of jalapeños."

"Maybe she'd never had a credit card set off so many bells and whistles before, and she was just going to find a supervisor and ask what to do."

"I'm not used to being treated like a criminal, Jonah. And to have my own father set me up like that—"

"The thing is, Katie, I can't imagine Jock completely shutting off your access to funds."

"I can," Kathryn said bitterly, "even though it's not his money I'm drawing on, it's my own. If he thought putting a hold on my credit card would be enough to bring me crawling home, he'd do it in a minute."

Jonah had gone straight on. "I'm betting that what the teller was supposed to do was quietly notify the head office before she processed the transaction, but then go ahead and let you have the money."

"Just do it slowly—stalling me till they could call Daddy?"

Jonah nodded. "It makes more sense than stopping you from using it, and Jock isn't dumb. Cut him a little slack, Katie. Whatever he did to that card, he didn't intend to get you arrested."

"You sound like you're defending him."

"No, I'm just trying to put myself in his shoes."

"I'm sure Daddy would appreciate the sympathy."

Jonah shot her an exasperated look. "I'm not justifying it, whatever he did. I'm trying to figure out what he'll do next."

"Call out the troops, probably. Now that he knows for certain where I am—"

"He knows where you *were,* but not where you *are.* As long as we stay on the move, we should be fine."

"Right. And you said we'd be perfectly safe walking into a bank this morning, too."

Jonah didn't answer. The silence lengthened, and Kathryn began to regret pushing the blame off on him. She hadn't been forced to agree to the plan, after all, so she bore equal responsibility for its failure.

"I'm sorry," she said quietly. "It's not your fault it didn't work."

A couple of minutes later Jonah pulled off the main street and into a supermarket parking lot. Rather than get out, he let the engine idle and stayed behind the wheel, turning to face Kathryn.

"Why are we stopping?" she asked, startled.

"We need to sort a few things out. You're worried, aren't you, Katie Mae?"

She nodded. "Aren't you?"

"I was for a couple of minutes in the bank, but not now that I've had a chance to think it over. The plan didn't go as smoothly as I hoped, but the fact is we've accomplished exactly what we set out to do—to make sure your father knows you're in Wisconsin. The difficult part is behind us now."

"But he also knows you're with me," she said quietly. "Complete with pictures from the security cameras."

"Yeah," Jonah admitted. "I was hoping you wouldn't think of that part just yet."

She bit her lip. "And that means you're marked, too."

"We knew it would happen sooner or later. In a way, it's a relief because we don't have an infinite set of scenarios to think about anymore."

"Just two people on the run, being chased by one very

powerful man who now knows exactly who and what he's looking for.''

"Your father's not psychic, Katie Mae. Don't give him credit for more power than he possesses, or you'll start making mistakes.''

"I'll try,'' she said wistfully. "I wish we'd managed to get our hands on some extra money, though.''

"It would make it easier,'' Jonah admitted. "It's going to be pretty tight, stretching what cash we have all the way to Nevada. We've got enough for gas and food, but nothing for luxuries—like motels along the way.''

"If the one we stayed in last night was a luxury, I'll sleep in the truck. I still have a backache from that mattress, and how you manage to be walking around at all after sleeping in that hollow…''

"The waking-up part was nice,'' he mused. "For a while, at least.''

She tried to will herself not to turn red.

"Anyway, don't fret about money. We'll make it.'' Jonah's voice held a careless note. "If we run low on cash, we can always sell your plaster model of West Podunk. I'm sure we'd have bidders standing eagerly in line for a treasure like that.''

"Don't, Jonah.'' Tears welled in her eyes. "I feel bad enough about that piece of foolishness already.''

"Oh, honey, I was just trying to make you laugh.'' He slid an arm around her and drew her close against him.

Kathryn bit her lip, and her voice trembled. "Do you think we should give it up right now?''

"Your father's not omnipotent, and we're not helpless.'' He pressed his lips against her hair. "But if you're having doubts… Katie—sweetheart—I'll do whatever you want, just tell me what it is. If you want to go home, just say the word.''

Home, she thought, almost bemused at the thought. But what was waiting for her at home, besides a furious father and a snake of an ex-fiancé? Another round of fortune hunters, probably, eager to tell her lies.

Kathryn tipped her head back against Jonah's shoulder so she could look up at him, into eyes that were dark and utterly sincere.

She had told him she'd rather marry an honest fortune hunter than take the chance of being fooled again. In truth, however, her description of the man she was seeking fit Jonah only halfway. He hadn't come around hunting for her money; he hadn't even leaped at the opportunity when she'd offered it. He'd thought it over and then made a decision. There was no denying that it had been a cool and calculated choice, and one that was definitely to his advantage. Still, he was a whole lot different from the fortune hunters she had encountered over the last few years.

But there was no doubt that Jonah fit the other half of the description. He had been honest....

She relaxed against him, and he pulled her closer and kissed her. Under the sweet persuasion of his lips, she felt her senses beginning to swirl and melt together until she was no longer certain of the difference between touch and taste, between sight and hearing. But she knew which sensations were Jonah, and she knew she didn't want to give up a single one of them.

''Jonah,'' she whispered. ''Take me to Nevada.''

''Right this minute?'' he murmured, and let his lips travel down the arch of her throat to the scoop neckline of her blouse.

"A little later will do," she managed.

And, after a while, he stopped kissing her and put the truck into gear.

At the first gas stop they made, Jonah thumbed through a rotating rack beside the convenience store's front door and picked out several highway maps. He'd already plotted the rough outlines of the trip in his head, but that basic route had been conjured up from memories, some more than a dozen years old. Now that they were traveling in earnest, he thought it was time to have a better plan.

Kathryn, who'd been looking at magazines, glanced over his shoulder with interest. "I thought we were going to watch every penny we spend. Do we need all of those?"

"And more. These are only the first few states we'll be crossing, but they don't have every map we'll need in stock here. I guess there's not much demand for Nevada maps in southern Wisconsin, because it's too far away."

"Too far away?" She eyed the stack with trepidation. "Jonah, how long is this trip really going to take?"

There was no point in minimizing the endurance contest which lay ahead of them. He might as well tell the truth—she had a right to know what she was in for. "Longer than I thought at first. Thirty hours or so of driving time."

"We're facing thirty hours of sitting in that truck?" She sounded horrified.

"Not all in one stretch, of course. We'll have to make stops along the way."

"All our teeth will be jolted loose by then, and my

legs will acquire a permanent kink from being bent around the cooler.''

''You'd better not insult the truck, Katie. It will not only take you to Nevada, it's going to bring you back again.''

She groaned. ''I'd forgotten that without my credit card I can't even fly home when this is over. Unless—Jonah, what if I was to call the company? It's my card, after all, and it's in my name. All I have to do is clear up the misunderstanding, and they'd issue me another card.''

''No problem at all. Except where are you going to have them mail it?''

''Damn. You know, my father has a lot to answer for. Just wait till the next time there's an important stockholders meeting and he wants my vote.''

''I still think you should phone him.''

''Only if you can route the call through Mars.''

''You don't have to have a heart-to-heart, just let him know you're all right.''

''After the funny business with the card, he doesn't deserve to know.''

Obviously she wasn't going to give in. Jonah shrugged. ''Grab a newspaper off that stack, Katie.''

Kathryn obliged, excusing herself to a woman who was standing beside the newspaper rack. ''Thirty hours,'' she muttered, folding the paper under her arm. ''Is it really that far to Nevada?''

''Didn't your family ever take a road trip through the great expanses of the country?''

She looked at him blankly.

Who was he kidding? Jonah asked himself. Of course they hadn't. It was difficult enough just to picture Jock

Campbell behind the wheel of a car, because he never drove himself when there was a chauffeur or an assistant or a bodyguard to do it. And it was utterly impossible to imagine him as an average working guy, driving straight through the night after a hard-earned week's vacation in the Rockies in order to get from Denver to northern Minnesota in time to go back to work on Monday morning, with the wife yawning over the road maps and the kids asleep in the back seat....

"You apparently weren't joking," he said dryly, "when you told me you weren't a great geography student, Katie Mae. Do you have any idea how many miles it is from here to Nevada?"

"In thirty hours," Kathryn said stubbornly, "we could go all the way across Europe by train."

"Great idea. Let's keep that in mind for the next time we elope. Or had you forgotten the main purpose of this trip?"

She wrinkled her nose. "Sorry."

It was, Jonah thought, one of her best tricks. He had to restrain himself from kissing the wrinkle away. "We could make better time on the major highways, but I think it's safer to stay on the side roads instead, at least till we're out of Wisconsin. Just think of it as taking the scenic route." He sidestepped a man who was inspecting the gummy worm display and dropped the maps beside the cash register, pulling out his wallet.

The clerk came across the store from where she'd been stocking bottled water in the refrigerators. "Which pump did you use, sir?"

Jonah waved a hand toward the window, where a half dozen vehicles stood beside the row of gasoline pumps.

"I didn't notice a number, but it's the blue truck over there."

"He means the one that used to be blue a long time ago," Kathryn added sweetly.

The clerk smiled while she counted out Jonah's change. "We get lots of those around here. Would you like all that stuff in a bag, ma'am?" Her eyebrows raised slightly as she glanced at Kathryn.

The clerk looked puzzled, Jonah thought in sudden consternation. Almost as if she'd seen something that reminded her of...

Hastily, he gathered up the maps and the newspaper. "Thanks, but we don't need a bag. Come on, honey, we need to get back on the road if we're going to make it to Chicago by tonight."

"What's the hurry?" Kathryn said as they crossed the asphalt to the truck. "You're practically running. We could have used a bag, you know, for all the litter we're collecting. And what's this about Chicago?"

"Didn't you notice the way she was looking at you?"

"What way?"

"As if she'd just been reminded of something important. Like—I'm guessing—your face." He handed her the newspaper. "You look, I'll drive." But he couldn't help glancing over her shoulder each time she turned a page. "There it is." He looked appraisingly from the newspaper photograph—a large color shot obviously taken from a formal portrait—to Kathryn. "I knew you should have cut your hair."

"And exactly when have I had time?" But Kathryn's voice had lost its cheerful bounce. "Now what do we do?"

It was an excellent question, Jonah thought. "We

keep right on with the plan,'' he said firmly. ''Maybe the clerk didn't recognize you. You were all dressed up for the picture that's in the paper, and you look a lot different wearing jeans and acting casual. Besides, we don't know that she even reads the newspaper, so it could have been just my imagination—thinking that she was looking at you at all.''

''You think perhaps she was simply admiring my expertise with eye shadow?'' Kathryn's voice was dry. ''Wishful thinking, Jonah.''

''Or even if she did notice the resemblance, maybe she'll get busy with the other people who were in the store and forget all about it. She can't have gotten a good enough look to be certain, and we didn't say anything where she could overhear us.''

Kathryn folded the newspaper and set it aside. ''Or maybe she'll call the toll-free number listed in the newspaper article and ask about the reward, just in case her suspicion turned out to be right.''

He wanted to swear. ''Jock's offered a reward? Damn. I suppose I should have expected that. But we can't run scared of everyone who lifts an eyebrow at us or we'll cause even more suspicion.''

''I'll remind you of that the next time you go rocketing out of a gas station as if the place is wired with high explosives,'' Kathryn muttered.

Jonah didn't bother to respond.

At the next stop, he chose the most distant gas pump and told Kathryn to stay in the truck. ''I can't even get out to stretch?'' she protested.

''Not until I've got you some kind of disguise.''

Her eyes narrowed. ''If you bring me a pair of sunglasses with a mustache attached, Clarke, I'll paste you to the concrete.''

He grinned. Inside the store, he looked around for anything that might conceal her resemblance to the newspaper photograph.

He was quite proud of his efforts, but it was with obvious trepidation that Kathryn opened the bag he handed her. First she pulled out a golf-style cap boasting the logo of a major restaurant chain—the main competitor of Katie Mae's Kitchens.

''The top of it's big enough to tuck all your hair into,'' he said. ''That's what they're designed for, to keep employees' hair out of the food.''

''I suppose I should be pleased they didn't stock babushkas,'' she muttered. ''And what's with the glasses?''

''I thought sunglasses would be a bit obvious, so I got the mildest reading glasses they had. Even with the clear lenses, that dark, heavy frame should draw attention away from those gorgeous blue eyes.'' He started the engine.

''And give me a major headache. Wait a minute— we're going on already? You're not even going to let me test out the disguise?''

''It would be a dead giveaway to walk into that store wearing the hat and glasses I just bought for you, Katie.''

She grumbled, but he drove on anyway. A few miles down the road she sat up straight and pointed out a roadside park. ''If I can't get out at the gas stations,'' she said, ''it's only fair that you stop and let me stretch my legs somewhere else.'' She grinned. ''Besides, now that I can't help with the driving, since I don't have a license, it will be extra important that you take breaks now and then.''

"If I didn't know better," Jonah grumbled, "I'd swear you left your license behind on purpose."

"We can have a picnic. Isn't there some kind of blanket in that first-aid kit we bought?"

He dug out the paper-thin emergency blanket while she gathered up sandwich makings and cold drinks, and followed her through scattered trees to a spot where sunlight fell onto thick green grass. She stopped so abruptly that Jonah almost ran into her, and he looked past her, over the edge of a bluff to a river which wended lazily through a green valley. "The Mississippi," he said. "Haven't you ever seen it before?"

"Of course. But from an airplane, it all looks flat."

He spread out the thin, foil-like blanket.

Kathryn walked toward the edge of the bluff. "It's so beautiful," she said. "So peaceful. Of course it's not as dramatic as the Rocky Mountains or the Grand Canyon—"

He frowned. "If you've seen the Rockies and the Canyon, Katie Mae, how can you not know how far away Nevada is?"

"Because we flew," she said simply.

And, he supposed, that explained it all. In an airplane, time passed—but there was no sense of distance or direction, as there was on the ground.

"But it has a glory all its own, doesn't it?" she went on. "All the shades of green...I wish I had a camera."

He was assembling ham and cheese into a monster of a sandwich. "Sorry I can't do anything to preserve this view, but if you're thinking of putting together a wedding album maybe we can order some prints of the two of us from the bank's security camera.''

''And there might be some video from that patrol car in Minnesota, too,'' she agreed cheerfully. She sat down next to him, cross-legged, and reached for a slice of ham. ''Jonah, what would you be doing today if we weren't here?''

He supposed he should have anticipated that she'd ask something of the sort, sooner or later. ''Working my regular shift.''

''What do you do?''

''I build electronic equipment.''

''Putting circuits together, you mean? That sounds tedious.''

''It can be. It's better than the plastics fabrication line I used to work on, because it's considerably less smelly. Before that I worked at a Katie Mae's in St. Paul.'' He finished his sandwich and lay back on the blanket, arms folded behind his head. ''I had a personal reference from your father to help me get that job, I'll have you know.''

From the corner of his eye he could see her toying with her ham, shredding it. ''Are you going to be in trouble with—what was your supervisor's name? Brian?—for not coming to work all week?''

In trouble? That was no doubt a mild way of putting it, Jonah thought. ''He'll probably have a few choice comments.'' The truth was that Brian was going to want to deep-fry him, but Jonah would deal with that problem when the time came.

''Don't forget to call him again. Jonah…''

He'd closed his eyes, and her voice seemed to be coming from a long way away. ''Yeah?''

"What reason are you going to give, for why you can't come to work?"

"Fishing," he said drowsily. "I'll tell him I've gone fishing."

What did it matter to her, Kathryn asked herself, whatever he told his boss? With the fifteen percent of Katie Mae's Kitchens that he was going to own, Jonah wouldn't need a job. He could go on a permanent, year-round fishing trip.

Or had he, half asleep as he'd been, meant something else altogether? Maybe he hadn't been talking about trout or bass but another kind of fish—something along the lines of a black-haired heiress?

Don't be silly, she told herself. If anyone had tossed out a lure, it had been her. She was letting her imagination get completely out of hand. No question about it, the sooner they got to Nevada and tied the knot, the better.

She packed up the picnic and sat quietly beside him for a few minutes, watching him sleep. But finally she stirred and reluctantly nudged him. "We've still got a long way to go, Jonah."

He sat up, rubbing his eyes, then stood up and pulled her to her feet.

Kathryn eyed the truck with disfavor. She hadn't even climbed in yet, but her backside was already protesting. "Split up over a couple of days, it won't be that bad," she told herself firmly. "Fifteen hours there, fifteen back…"

Jonah shook his head. "It's thirty hours each way. I thought I told you that."

"Each way?" Her voice was little more than a

squeak. "Just pass the sleeping pills and wake me when we get there, all right?"

But the scenery helped to pass the time. They followed the Great River Road for a while, down the edge of the Mississippi. And when they cut off across country again, still following the side roads, they drove through small towns and villages that delighted her with their Victorian charm, their small tidy houses and businesses that all seemed to carry the town's name. Only reluctantly did she stop looking at buildings and get out the road map when Jonah asked her to check on their progress.

"I think we're far enough away now that we can risk using the major highways," he said. "So if you'll plot a route to connect up with the interstate—"

She ran a finger along the map. "Where are we, anyway?"

"I haven't been paying much attention. Still in Iowa, I think."

"Then this must be Ash Grove. There's a highway running straight west that should take us directly—" She looked up, hoping to see a sign that would identify the town, and gasped. "I don't believe it. A farmers' market and everything. This is like a picture postcard!"

Ahead of them was a wedding cake of a courthouse, standing majestically alone in the center of a parklike square. In the streets around it, trucks and vans were parked, doors open to show off the colorful bounty of early summer's garden produce. Facing the courthouse all around were businesses, lined up in neat rows like tin soldiers on parade. Late-afternoon sun fell across the scene, producing a soft, warm light that would have made Hollywood burn with envy.

"Very nice," Jonah said dryly. "Where am I supposed to turn?"

"Up there, I think." Kathryn pointed. "If I'm reading this map right, there should be a sign just past the square."

"What do you mean, if you're reading the map right? You know, Katie, at times like this I wish you hadn't told me about your geography grades."

The stoplight turned green and the truck eased into the intersection, both of them looking for the signs that should mark their turn.

That was why neither of them saw the car that came hurtling through the intersection against the light and smashed into the left front corner of the pickup truck.

CHAPTER SIX

THE only warning Jonah had was the sound of brakes shrieking a bare instant before the impact spun the truck sideways across the highway, almost shoving it into a van parked at the corner of the courthouse square. There was no time to dodge the oncoming car, or even to brace himself against the shock, much less to try to cushion Kathryn from the crash. As the truck came to rest, upright but still rocking wildly, he was almost afraid to look at her.

If she was injured, after putting herself into his care... She'd argued against buying the damned truck, but he'd insisted. If his decision had ended up hurting her...

But apart from looking shaken and a bit dazed, she appeared to be all right. There were no obvious bumps and bruises, no blood streaming down her face. "Are you all right?" he asked.

She didn't answer.

He said, more urgently, "Dammit, Katie, are you hurt?"

She shook her head a little as if to clear it. "No. I'm fine. You can relax, Jonah—I'm not going to die on you before you get your fifteen percent of Katie Mae's."

The woman must have ice in her veins, he thought irritably, if that was the first thing she thought of. "Good," he growled. "Though that wasn't what was worrying me at the moment. I was having a nightmare

95

flash of having to explain what happened to your father.''

"What *did* happen? What hit us?''

He looked out through the cracked windshield over the smashed-in hood, surveying the car which had wrapped itself around the corner of the truck. "It looks like an old Cadillac.''

"Well, that figures. It would take a big car to hurt this tank.''

"Just be glad we weren't driving a compact or they'd be cutting us out of it with blowtorches," Jonah said. "Maybe we should check whether the other driver is all right.''

Kathryn leaned across him to take a look. "And exactly how do you plan to do that when my door won't open and yours has a car folded up against it? I suppose the good news is that the doors now match—neither of them works right.''

She had a point, Jonah admitted. He tried his window and was relieved when it rolled down properly.

For a little town, he realized, it suddenly seemed to be remarkably full of people.

The entire group at the farmers' market, vendors and customers alike, were crowding around. The man who'd been tending the van they'd almost hit was trying to extract the driver from the Cadillac. Another man, after a long look at the driver's side of the truck, walked around to the passenger side, pulled out a pocket knife, and began slicing away at the duct tape blocking Kathryn's door. A moment later he had the door open and was offering his hand to her. "Sorry about the way we greeted you, ma'am. We don't generally treat strangers quite so roughly around here.''

"And here I thought that was the welcome wagon rushing to greet us!"

The humor in Kathryn's voice sounded a little forced. Maybe, Jonah thought, she wasn't quite so levelheaded as she'd like to pretend, after all. His irritation died away.

Jonah slid out after her. The smell of hot brakes and burnt rubber hung in a cloud around the wreck, but he thought he could detect yet another odor, as well. Bending down, he eyed the green puddle of antifreeze which was forming under the front of the truck. It shouldn't be any surprise that the radiator had ruptured, he told himself, and added another day to his mental estimate of how long it would take to get back on the road.

The man who had helped them out of the truck pushed his hat farther back on his head. "The junkyard will be sending along a tow truck pretty soon."

"Junkyard?" Jonah said.

The man grinned. "Sorry. I forgot you wouldn't know it's the body shop, too."

"Thanks for calling them."

"Oh, nobody called. They'll just be along as soon as the word spreads. A couple of the guys went down to get the fire engine, too, so they can hose down the mess." He held out a hand. "I'm the mayor of Ash Grove. Larry Benson's the name."

Jonah didn't see any graceful way to avoid introducing himself. "Jonah Clarke."

"And Mrs. Clarke?" The mayor's gaze drifted toward Kathryn, who had joined the crowd around the Cadillac. "That's quite a lady you've got there—most women would be in hysterics by now, getting in a smash like this. Quite a ways from home, too—I see by your license plate you're from Minnesota.''

"Yeah," Jonah said. He eyed the Cadillac's driver, still sitting behind the wheel. "Will the ambulance be along soon, too?"

"Doubt we'll need it. She's the *other* sort of woman."

Obviously the mayor thought she was the hysterical sort. "Do you know her?"

"Oh, heck, yes. She's always driving like a maniac."

"I hope she's all right."

"Her own fault if she isn't," the mayor said. "The way she's carrying on, I'd say there isn't much doubt of it. She'll quit as soon as she realizes the act won't do her any good. Plenty of people saw what really happened."

"I'm not sure myself," Jonah admitted.

"She'll probably say the sun was in her eyes—and at this time of day, it can be. But she knows perfectly well that stoplight's there, and she ran it big as... Here's the town constable. He'll get to the bottom of it."

Just what we need, Jonah thought. Any constable worth his salt would automatically check the record of any driver involved in an accident, no matter which one caused it. And when the file came back... *We're really in the soup now.*

"Don't worry about it, son," the mayor said. "It wasn't your fault. We'll see that you're fixed up as good as..." He paused as his gaze came to rest on the banged-up truck. "Well, maybe not quite as good as *new,* now that I stop to think about it, but—"

The constable interrupted to ask for Jonah's driver's license, and he was tied up for a while answering questions and signing reports. By the time he was finished, the woman in the Cadillac had finally climbed out. She was mopping at a scrape on her forehead, and he heard her say something about plastic surgery.

He circled through the crowd to avoid coming into contact with her and joined Kathryn at one of the food stalls, where she seemed to be inspecting the produce.

She looked up with a question in her eyes, but instead of asking it, she said mildly, "Nice lettuce they grow here. Still, I was only making a general comment about the farmers' market. It really wasn't necessary to go to these lengths to give me a closer look, Jonah."

"And here I thought you'd be pleased." He looked closer. "You forgot your hat and glasses."

She looked momentarily disconcerted, then she shrugged. "Too late now."

She was right, he thought. If any of the citizens of Ash Grove were likely to recognize her, the mischief was already done; every soul in town must be gathered in the square by now, gawking at the accident and the strangers. "The tow truck is supposed to be along shortly."

"How bad is the damage, Jonah?"

He couldn't quite meet her eyes. "We won't be going anywhere tonight, that's sure. The mayor has offered to drive you up to the motel. There appears to be only one in town."

Kathryn eyed him levelly. "What about you?"

"I'll go with the tow truck and find out what I can."

"You're rubbing the side of your head."

"It's nothing. I must have bumped it on the door when we spun around."

"You should have an ice pack on it." She turned

toward the truck. "There's still some ice in the cooler, I'm sure. I'll just have to find a plastic bag to put it in."

"Skip it, Katie. Here's the tow truck. Better grab your clothes." He stepped away to watch as the wrecker pulled the Cadillac away with a screech of metal and towed it off down the street.

A moment later a frigid little hand tugged at his sleeve, and Kathryn handed him a bag full of ice, wrapped in the hat he'd intended as her disguise. "See? I had plenty of time."

He gave in and laid the ice pack above his ear. "You don't want to keep the mayor waiting."

"Jonah," she said. "You will be coming to the motel, won't you?"

"Sure," he said. "As soon as I can."

She gave him a long, steady look, and then rummaged behind the seat of the truck till she'd gathered up their possessions. She handed the two brown paper bags which contained their clothes to the mayor with as much dignity as if she'd been presenting him with mono-grammed leather luggage.

The woman had class, Jonah thought. There was no denying that much—even though in the space of forty-eight hours she'd gone from a mansion to a series of rundown motels, from a fancy wedding gown to a pair of resale-shop jeans, from spending a honeymoon in Bermuda to being stranded in Ash Grove, Iowa, with no transportation and little cash.

Taking up with him, he thought irritably, had not ex-actly improved Katie Mae Campbell's life.

The motel was only a few blocks from the square, and Mayor Benson spent the short drive telling Kathryn about Ash Grove. "It's not much more than a wide spot in the road, of course. But it's a *nice* wide spot."

He parked in front of the Highway Motel. Kathryn vaguely remembered seeing it as she and Jonah had passed by less than an hour before. She'd noticed it because of the pleasant front porch and the slatted wooden swing which hung there, but she hadn't expected ever to see it again. *So much for making plans.*

The mayor didn't get out of the car but sat for a moment drumming his fingertips on the steering wheel. "If you're in bad circumstances," he said finally, without looking at her, "the town has a small fund for people with emergencies. I could get you some money."

The offer touched Kathryn's heart and brought a mist to her eyes.

"It's not meant as charity, you understand," he added hastily. "But having an accident and all, far away from home—unexpected expenses—anybody can get in an embarrassing spot."

"Thank you, Mr. Benson," she managed. "I think we'll be all right for a day or two."

"Well, you let me know if you need anything. I'll take you in now, introduce you to Jennie and Sam."

The office was empty, and it was several minutes after Mayor Benson rang the bell on the front desk before a woman came in, walking stiffly and leaning heavily on a cane. "Hello, Larry. The girls at the hardware store called to tell me you were headed this way." Her bright blue eyes focused on Kathryn's face, appearing not to notice the brown paper bag in her arms. "Sorry to hear about your misfortune, my dear. We'll do all we can, Sam and I, to make you comfortable, but I'm afraid the accommodations are nothing grand, especially now that my arthritis has kicked up and Sam's angina is bothering him again.''

"I'm sure we'll be quite comfortable, Mrs...."

"Just Jennie will do, dear. Come on back into the kitchen. The tea should be ready by now, I started the kettle when the girls called. You can go away now, Larry, I'll take it from here. Thanks for bringing her over." She led the way through a door at the back of the office. "What's your name, dear?"

Fleetingly, Kathryn considered possible aliases, but concluded that if she tried to change her name at this stage she'd trip herself up for certain. So she told the truth.

"It's a pretty name," Jennie said. "I thought the girls at the hardware store said it was Clarke, but never mind. They're always getting things mixed up."

"That's...my fiancé's name."

Jennie's left eyebrow tilted a little. "Oh, really?"

Great, Kathryn thought. *Here's where you get thrown out on your ear with a lecture about immoral behavior. Traveling across the country with a man you're not married to...*

Why hadn't she remembered in time that she was squarely in the middle of small-town America? What harm would it have done to let the woman assume they were married? A day or two and they'd be gone, anyway.

At the moment, Kathryn told herself, she could have put the ice bag she'd concocted for Jonah to good use on her own aching head. This was all getting much too complicated.

*　　*　　*

It was more than an hour before Jonah arrived; darkness had already fallen and the evening air was beginning to cool. Kathryn admitted to feeling relieved when she saw him get out of a car in front of the motel and stride up the walk toward the front porch swing where she sat. He was carrying the cooler, and he had a bundle tucked under one arm.

He paused with one foot propped on the top step. "I thought you'd be getting settled. Was there a problem with getting a room?"

Only the one I almost caused. "No problem. It just doesn't take long to unpack a paper bag. Especially when I don't know how long we'll be here."

He put the cooler down, handed her the bundle, and came to sit next to her in the swing.

Kathryn looked at the bundle in her lap. She didn't have to open the plastic bag or strip away the tissue paper to know what she was holding—he'd brought her souvenir model of the West Podunk truck stop. But why hadn't he just left it under the truck seat instead of carting it across town? Surely not out of concern that it would turn up missing from the body shop. Which meant...

"It's not good news, then," she said. "They can't repair the truck—that's why you cleaned it out. Right? I'm surprised you didn't bring the fuzzy dice. You seemed quite taken with them."

"They're in the cooler. A good body shop can repair almost anything, with enough time and money. But the easiest way to fix our truck would be to cut it in two right behind the cab, then throw the front half away and weld on a new one."

"Not very practical." It took effort, but she managed

to keep her voice from trembling. "Especially on our budget."

He nodded. "Even if the young woman's insurance company pays up, it'll take some time. And I wouldn't want to bet on how much they'll offer."

"So...now what?"

Jonah took a deep breath. "I think it's time to throw in the towel."

"You want to stop even thinking about going to Nevada." She was almost relieved. Unless... What, precisely, did he mean by that? Was he canceling out the long drive, or the whole idea of marriage?

"It's not realistic, honey. I don't know what I was thinking of. Trying to drive that far, without proper rest...it's too dangerous. You could have been hurt today."

"The accident wasn't your fault, Jonah."

"Give me another long day behind the wheel and it could have been. I think we should take it as a warning and stop before we get ourselves in serious trouble."

She asked carefully, "So if we're not going to Nevada, what will we do instead?"

"You don't mind?"

"I don't regret missing out on the long ride, if that's what you mean. I just wondered what the alternate plan was."

"I hadn't gotten that far yet," he admitted.

She hesitated. "Has anything else changed?"

"Like what?"

"I thought maybe fifteen percent of Katie Mae's Kitchens was beginning to lose its appeal to you, considering what you've had to go through so far."

A smile tugged at the corner of his mouth. "So you're

wondering if I've thought better of the offer? No, Katie. I'd still marry you in a minute if it was possible.''

It was rather sweet of him to put it that way, she thought. It was a good thing they had a clear understanding, however—for otherwise it might be tempting to forget that it was Katie Mae's Kitchens, and not only Kathryn herself, that he intended to marry.

She tried to keep her voice casual. ''Then how about in three days?''

''What are you talking about?''

''That's how long it takes to get a marriage license here. No blood tests, no extra rigmarole. Apply for the license, wait three days, pick it up, get married. That's all there is to it. And since we're not going to get the truck back, it'll probably take us that long to figure out how we're going to get home, anyway.''

''How do you know all this?'' He sounded half suspicious.

''The motel owner told me.''

''Katie, how did she even find out that you were interested in the subject?''

She told herself that there was no need for him to know the details about Jennie's delicate questions, her own storm of tears, the woman's soothing touch and soft voice and deep concern. So she dodged the question. ''You may have noticed that people in this town are not particularly good at minding their own business.'' The comment, true though it was, made her feel a little disloyal to Jennie. ''I mean—well, they're not nasty about it, or gossipy. I suppose they only want to help.''

''Yeah, I'd gathered that everybody's interested.'' His voice was dry. ''The guy at the body shop was dying to know the details, too. In fact, he offered me a job if we decide to stick around." He brushed the back of his hand against her cheek. "Sure, Katie Mae—I can't think of anything I'd rather do this week than hang around Ash Grove and marry you."

Kathryn let out a breath she hadn't realized she'd been holding.

"Let's walk over to the supermarket and celebrate," he said.

She smiled. "Is that the hot spot in town?"

"I suppose so. At least it seems to be the only place to get something to eat. Now that we're not watching our pennies for gas all the way to Nevada—heck, we can spring for a hamburger *and* fries without breaking the budget."

"Is there anything in the cooler that needs to be taken care of?"

Jonah shook his head. "I don't think there's anything worth saving. After you took all the ice to soothe my wounded head, it seems like the safest thing to do."

"Then just leave it here, and we'll pick it up on the way back. Jennie put us way at the far end of the motel."

"She's worried about our privacy *before* the wedding?" Jonah sounded delighted.

"She did say nobody would bother us back there," Kathryn admitted, "but also the room has a few extras."

"Hot tub?" he speculated. "Waterbed? Satin sheets? This woman is setting a new standard for helpfulness."

"Don't get your hopes up too far," Kathryn advised.

As they walked through the soft summer night, it seemed perfectly natural that Jonah reached for her hand. The scent of roses drifted toward them from the gardens they passed, and even the occasional grinding noise of an eighteen-wheeler passing on the highway didn't drown out the soft songs of the evening birds and the calls of mothers summoning their children home from play.

"I'm sorry about the truck coming to such a bad end," Kathryn admitted. "I was actually starting to get fond of the old thing."

"So was I—even if it was getting just two hundred miles to a quart of oil."

"Funny you didn't mention that earlier."

"You know perfectly well why I didn't."

"Because I'd have thrown a fit and said it wasn't safe."

He smiled down at her. "Yes, but in the end you'd have climbed back in anyway. You know, Katie, you're a sport. I can't think of another woman who'd handle this whole thing the way you have."

And considering the number of women he must know, Kathryn thought, that was really a compliment.

So why didn't she feel especially good about it?

By the time they came back from the supermarket, the motel was dark except for a couple of units, but Jonah noticed there were only a few cars in the parking lot. "I wonder where everyone is," he mused. "We obviously didn't find the local excitement after all."

"There are only a few people staying here."

He was puzzled. "But there must be twenty rooms, and the No Vacancy sign is lit."

"It was when Mayor Benson brought me over, too. Jennie and Sam aren't taking very many guests these days, and when they reach their limit, they turn the sign on. Our situation apparently stimulated her curiosity."

"And a good thing, too." Jonah retrieved the cooler

from under the porch swing where they'd left it and they walked the length of the motel to the farthest unit. Inside, he looked around with interest. ''I see why you told me not to get excited at the idea of extra features.''

''Hey, we're coming up in the world. We have our own kitchen now—if you can call it that when it consists of a two-burner hotplate, a sink that's hardly big enough to set a cup in, and a refrigerator that might hold a half gallon of milk if you put it in sideways.''

Jonah kissed her temple. ''And I have three days to check out what kind of cook you are before *I* do anything irrevocable,'' he murmured. ''I can't wait.''

She was asleep—or pretending to be—when he finished his shower. She'd left a bedside lamp turned on, and he watched her as he toweled his hair dry. There was one sure way to tell, he decided, and slid under the blanket beside her, nestling against her warmth. If she was awake, she couldn't possibly keep from responding to his touch—even if it was only by an involuntary tensing.

But she merely sighed, and after a moment he reflected that it was hardly fair to be feeling lustful when she was dead tired. Besides, he reminded himself, that hadn't been the point of the test at all. Not that he couldn't go make his phone call whether or not she was awake; it would just cause fewer questions if he waited until she was sound asleep.

So he might as well wait right here—warm and comfortable, with his nose pressed against her sweet-scented hair…for a little while.

Only after he was certain she was dead to the world did he slide out of bed and into his clothes once more.

The pay phone he'd noticed at the corner of the motel

parking lot was under a tree, but a nearby street lamp cast just enough light that he could see to dial the zillion numbers it took to use his phone card. After a half dozen rings, the telephone was answered with a sort of grunt.

Jonah glanced at his watch and grinned. "Hello, Brian," he said clearly.

"Hey, buddy—where are you?"

"Still in the central time zone."

Brian snorted. "That just means you know quite well it's an ungodly hour to be calling me."

"You must have had a really tough day. I can hang up and stop bothering you."

"No! I don't suppose you want to tell me what you're up to this time?"

"That's not why I'm calling, no."

"I see. Is she a blonde, a brunette, or a redhead?"

Jonah grinned. "None of the above. I don't see why you always assume there's a woman involved."

"Because there generally is."

"Hey, seriously—has anybody been around asking questions about me?"

"Only the usual crowd," Brian said airily, "and I've been telling them we had to commit you to a top-secret detox hospital in California to get you off the booze and drugs."

Jonah's voice was dry. "Thanks, Brian, you're a real pal."

"Come on, man, get real. I hate to bruise your ego, but hardly anybody noticed that you took the day off. Just don't go getting the idea you can disappear for weeks."

"Well, if anybody comes nosing around asking about me…"

"Want to give me a hint as to who these suspicious characters might be?"

"No, except that one of them might be my father. Just tell them everything you know."

"But you haven't said a damned thing, Jonah!"

"Then you won't have any trouble remembering what to tell them, will you? I'll talk to you again in a couple of days."

He hung up and stood for a moment in indecision, rubbing his jaw. Then he pulled a folded scrap of newspaper out of his pocket and picked up the phone again.

He'd put this off as long as he could. Now it had to be done.

It was a faint meow that woke Kathryn, but she wasn't certain at first whether it was real or in her dreams. She raised up on one elbow and heard it again, outside the window at the front of the room.

She glanced at Jonah, whose face was buried in his pillow, and slid out of bed. A few minutes later she was sitting on the edge of the porch in front of their room, watching a scrawny tabby kitten attacking a scrap of deli ham that she'd salvaged from the cooler, when Jonah opened the door.

"You're up early," he said. "Who's your friend? And don't tell me she's just a stray, because you know perfectly well that if you feed her she's going to be stuck to you like glue." He sat down next to her on the step, picked up another scrap of ham, and let it dangle from between his fingers.

"You're a fine one to talk," she gibed. "What did Brian say when you called him last night?"

"That I hadn't been missed much," he said easily, "and that he'll keep covering for me as long as he can."

The kitten swallowed the last morsel, daintily licked her paw, and crouched, eyeing the bit of ham in Jonah's fingers. He toyed with it, swinging his hand, and the kitten's head turned in perfect synchronization.

"You could have called him from the room."

"I didn't want to disturb you. But I guess I did anyway, didn't I? The lamp was turned on when I left, off when I came back."

The kitten crept closer and stretched out a paw, and Jonah handed over the ham.

"Let's get dressed," he said. "We've got important errands to run this morning. We'll need to pick up some milk for the cat. Oh, and there's a little matter of a marriage license, too."

The courthouse that looked like a wedding cake was just as ornate on the inside; the offices had twelve-foot ceilings, elaborate plaster work, and marble counters.

The clerk who waited on them was obviously delighted by the experience. "The whole town feels bad that you couldn't finish your trip," she confided, "but it's so exciting that you've decided to get married here instead. I'm so pleased to be part of it." She bustled around the office and slapped a sheet of paper on the counter in front of them. "Here's the application form. You just fill it out as it directs."

Simple enough, Kathryn thought.

"Don't sign yet, though," the clerk cautioned, "because there has to be a notary to swear to your signatures. I'll have to call Rosalie from upstairs. Then we just need a witness—but I see you've brought Jennie along—and the processing fee."

Kathryn reached for a pen. Jonah began to count out the fee.

"And I'll need to see a driver's license for each of you, of course."

Kathryn was concentrating on the form, so it took an instant for the clerk's announcement to sink in.

"What did you say?" she breathed. "You need to see *what?*"

Jonah put his elbows on the counter and dropped his face into his hands. "Your driver's license," he groaned.

The driver's license she had left behind in their rush to get out of the bank in Madison.

This absolutely cannot be happening, Kathryn thought. *It isn't possible.*

Helplessly and hopelessly, she started to laugh at the utter craziness of it. And then she began to cry.

CHAPTER SEVEN

As Kathryn began to weep, Jonah lifted his face out of his hands. At the moment, he thought, she sounded more frustrated than anything else, but it wouldn't take much to turn her defeated sobs into a full-blown case of hysterics. He didn't blame her. In fact, if he'd thought it would do any good, he'd have been tempted to join her.

Instead, he put his arms around her, and she huddled against him more tightly than he'd thought possible, her face buried in his neck. The corner of her purse, still slung from her shoulder, dug uncomfortably into his midriff. But dislodging it would mean letting go of her, and in her present state of mind she'd probably take that as rejection. So he braced himself against the discomfort and leaned his cheek on her hair. "Hang on, Katie," he said. "We'll figure something out."

The clerk looked baffled by the storm she'd set off. "It's only a formality," she said helplessly. "Especially around here, where we know everyone. Actually, the driver's license is just to prove that you're really who you say you are, because the law says we have to check your legal name."

Jonah muttered, "Bringing along a witness isn't enough?"

The clerk stood her ground. "Begging your pardon, sir, but Jennie hasn't known you any longer than the rest of us have. She's taking your word for it all."

113

Jennie said gently, "Yes, I am. I'm quite sure if these young people were playing games with the truth, we wouldn't be here this morning."

"But I can't do that," the clerk said doggedly, "or I'd lose my job. I have to look at some kind of identification that includes a photo—like a driver's license."

Kathryn sniffed. *At least she's stopped crying,* he thought.

"Besides, everybody has a driver's license," the clerk said. "Don't they?"

In a rural area like this, Jonah thought, without the kind of mass transportation available in cities, she was probably right—everybody who was old enough learned to drive a car. Not that the fact was any help to them, under the circumstances.

Kathryn huddled closer. The purse jabbed him harder. He frowned, then gently pushed Kathryn away, which relieved the pressure on his rib, and took hold of her purse.

For such a tiny thing, it was amazingly full of compartments—at least six of them, each closed off by a separate zipper or snap. And it was stuffed full, he realized as he opened the first section.

Methodically, he started emptying the purse onto the marble counter. Lipstick, mirror, comb…a bundle of keys….a pen and matching mechanical pencil, each with her initials engraved on the clip…a neatly folded handkerchief…two twenties and three one-dollar bills…a tube of hand lotion…two pieces of peppermint candy…a nail file and emery board…the cash register receipt for her crazy souvenir from West Podunk…a small white envelope…

"What's that?" she said, reaching for it.

"You don't even know everything you're carrying around?" He handed it over and turned back to his task, pulling out a slim gold case full of business cards. Just as quickly, he tucked it away again, hoping that no one else had seen the logo of Katie Mae's Kitchens stamped on the front. Why had she been taking those on her honeymoon, anyway?

"How do women ever find anything in these silly little bags you insist on carrying?" he grumbled.

Kathryn had opened the envelope and pulled out a slip of light blue paper. "Well, that's pretty useless," she muttered and shoved it back into the envelope. She reached for the handkerchief he'd laid aside and dabbed at her eyes. "If you wouldn't mind telling me what you're looking for, Jonah, maybe I can tell you where to find it."

"It has to be here somewhere. You told me you brought it, and there's nowhere else you could keep it safe." He tugged impatiently at another zipper. "Your passport, Katie. You told me you had it because you were on your way to..." Almost too late, he remembered their very attentive audience. "Never mind. But you must still have it somewhere."

Kathryn's eyes widened. "I'd forgotten all about it." She reached for the handbag and from a concealed pocket deep inside, she drew out a dark blue folder. "Imagine that. Douglas turned out to be good for something after all." She looked up at him with relief and gratitude. "Jonah, you're marvelous!"

Jonah shook his head in astonishment as he surveyed the assortment spread out on the counter. "I'd have sworn I emptied every corner of that thing. What's wrong with ordinary pockets, anyway? Men never have all this trouble locating something.''

''That,'' the clerk said, ''is because a man gives anything important to his wife and says, 'Here, honey, put this in your purse.'''

Jennie laughed. ''You're right. Sam does it all the time.''

''Let me take a look at that.'' The clerk reached for the passport. ''We don't see many of these around here, but as long as it's official and has a picture…'' She glanced speculatively from the photograph to Kathryn's face. ''This doesn't look as much like you as the one in the newspaper does.''

Jonah stopped breathing. Kathryn seemed to freeze beside him. ''What newspaper?'' he asked.

''The Ash Grove *Advocate,*'' the clerk said. ''It comes out only twice a week, and your accident was such big news they held up the presses last night so they could get a picture in of all the damage.'' She copied the number off the passport and goggled for a moment at the multicolored stamps which filled the pages before handing it back. ''Sorry, I didn't mean to be nosy, looking through it like that. But have you really been to all those places?''

Kathryn nodded. ''Though it feels like a million years ago.''

''I'd like to visit just one of them someday,'' the clerk said gloomily. ''Any one of them would do. But what I don't understand is, if you've been all over the world, why you were driving through Ash Grove in an old pickup tr—''

Jennie cleared her throat firmly.

The clerk turned red. ''Sorry. None of my business.''

"But of course you're curious," Kathryn said. She started to gather up her possessions. "This is...well, we're just having an adventure."

"I see," said the clerk, who obviously didn't. "Well, if you'll finish the application form..."

Kathryn finished stuffing everything back in her handbag and picked up the pen.

After all the uproar, Jonah wouldn't have been surprised if her hands had trembled as she filled in the blanks, but she appeared steady as a rock. She finished and handed him the pen.

"For better or worse," she murmured. "And, of course, I'm not forgetting the fifteen percent."

He hesitated, the pen poised above the document. Beside the question *Name After Marriage,* he noted, she had written Kathryn Mae Clarke. It was as neat and precise as if she'd practiced it. Or as if the whole idea of changing her name hadn't caused her to turn a hair.

He wondered if she felt the same way about changing her life.

We're just having an adventure, his soon-to-be bride had said. Did that mean she didn't intend this marriage to make any real difference at all?

The courthouse was only a few blocks from the Highway Motel, but because of Jennie's arthritis she'd insisted that they drive her car. Once it was safely back in the garage and the old woman had gone inside the motel office, Kathryn sat down in the porch swing and drew up her feet, wrapping her arms around her knees. "What now?" she said. "What are we supposed to do with ourselves till Friday?"

The obvious answer hit her just a little too late to call

back the words, and she was certain Jonah wouldn't miss it. Two people who were already sharing a room and a bed generally didn't need much extra entertainment in order to pass the time. The only real question, she supposed, was how he'd phrase the invitation to make love.

But to her surprise, Jonah didn't seem to notice. "We'd better take another look at the finances. Between the motel bill and the judge's fee, by the end of the week we may be scraping bottom."

It was silly, she told herself, to be disappointed that he hadn't jumped at her naive question. Much easier this way, especially since she would have turned him down anyway.

Wouldn't she?

"Too bad we can't use the check you found in my bag this morning," she said. "It would eliminate all our current money worries and then some."

"Is that what was in the envelope?"

"Ten grand." Kathryn let the phrase roll over her tongue. She could almost taste it. "Daddy must have tucked it in my bag as a surprise."

"Spending money for Bermuda? Quite a nice surprise."

"Except it's a cashier's check made out to Douglas and me jointly, so unless you feel like forging his name, it's no good at all to us."

He didn't seem to hear. "I still think you should call your father, Katie."

She looked at him in exasperation. "And do what? Invite him to the wedding? Jonah, there's no sense in asking for trouble. It's going to be bad enough as it is when we break the news that we're married."

"The news," he said softly, "that you've married the gardener's son. Is that what you mean?"

Kathryn was stunned. "No, it's not. I doubt my father would be happy right now, whoever I married. He'll probably think I'm on the rebound and you've snapped me up without giving me a chance to think."

"Aren't you? And haven't I?"

"Of course not," she snapped. "But you can't expect Daddy to understand our reasons."

"You mean *your* reasons," he said wryly. "Marrying a fortune hunter to avoid being pursued by fortune hunters... You know, I can understand why Jock might have a little trouble with that logic."

"Exactly. And though your reason is a little more easily explained, you can't expect him to like it any better."

"Now that you mention it," Jonah mused, "I can't quite picture Jock Campbell congratulating me for negotiating a prenuptial agreement that includes fifteen percent of Katie Mae's Kitchens."

"That's why letting him find out about this would be crazy, because if he thinks there's a ghost of a chance of stopping us, he'd swoop down like a vulture. And now that we can't run any farther, we'd be carrion just lying there waiting for him. So—"

The door of the motel office rattled, and Jonah pulled it open and helped Jennie maneuver a small cart of linens and cleaning supplies outside.

"Will you be out of your room for a little while?" she asked pleasantly. "It'll take me about an hour to clean it, I'm afraid. I don't move as quickly as I used to."

Kathryn looked across her to Jonah. The look of shock on his face must be mirrored on her own, she thought.

It had never occurred to her that Jennie didn't have a team of chambermaids, or that limiting the number of guests at the motel was because the physical demands of taking care of them were too much for her to handle.

"Go back inside," Kathryn said crisply. "And leave the cart here. When I'm finished cleaning our room, I'll do the others. You might make a list of the room numbers and what needs doing, so I don't miss anything."

Jennie protested, but when Jonah threatened to carry her back into the office, she finally capitulated. Jonah held the door for her and came back to stand on the porch, hands on hips, looking speculatively at Kathryn. "I was joking about you having to scrub floors to pay our way."

"Good, because if she tries to pay me, I'll turn it down. The truth is, just because I have a maid, you believe I don't know anything about being one. You don't think I can do the work, do you?"

"I think you can probably do anything you set your mind to, Katie."

"My father used to tell me that you should never miss an opportunity to learn a new skill, because you don't know when some experience and a reference might come in handy." She dropped into step beside him as Jonah pushed the cart down the walk toward the far end of the building. "Besides, it occurs to me that I may go home without a job, too."

"Jock wouldn't really fire you, would he?"

She shot a glance up at him. "If he does," she said deliberately, "it will be for displaying bad judgment— not for marrying the gardener's son."

"In Jock's mind, there may not be much of a difference between the two. Is that why you're doing this, Katie?''

"You mean, do I see myself marrying some sort of peasant just to annoy my father? No, Jonah. This isn't about my father, and I don't think of you as the gardener's son. There's something about you...."

She had never stopped to think about it before. And even now that she had, Kathryn couldn't put her finger on exactly what it was about him that made him so different. An air of self-confidence, perhaps. She hadn't realized how much a part of him that was, until now—when for the first time she saw him displaying a hint of doubt about himself and his abilities.

And there was that aura of kindness about him that always left her feeling warm and comforted and safe....

Beside the door of their room, the scrawny kitten huddled under a ragged rosebush. The twin dishes of milk and cat food that Kathryn had set out before they left for the courthouse had both been licked clean, and the kitten was cleaning her whiskers. She stopped when she saw them, however, and uttered a pitifully weak meow.

"You little fraud," Kathryn said. "You can't still be starving. I gave you a whole can of cat food and I can see your tummy bulging, so I know no other cat came along and beat you up for it.''

Jonah squatted down and held out a hand. "Come here, Sigmund Fraud.'' The kitten crept out from under the bush to lay a pleading paw on his wrist.

"Now that's outrageous," Kathryn said. "I'm the one that feeds her, but she won't even let me touch her—she comes to you instead. I realize that you have a certain charm for the ladies, Jonah, but enough is enough.''

Jonah grinned. An instant later, with a move almost

too fast to see, he picked up the kitten by the scruff of the neck. "Here," he said cheerfully. "You can hold her."

Kathryn took one look at the four sets of claws the kitten had bared and stepped back. "No, thanks. Not till you've tamed her a little more."

"My feelings are hurt," he said mournfully. "Just a minute ago you were offended that she prefers me, but now you want to take advantage of my talent."

He set the kitten down. Kathryn expected the animal to scurry back under the rosebush, but instead she sat down indignantly in the center of the sidewalk and began to wash.

"Though I'm apparently not as much of a hit as you thought," Jonah said, "since she's now scrubbing my scent off her fur."

Kathryn sniffed. "It would serve you right if every female you tried to charm acted the same way."

"By taking baths in public? Now that would be a hit."

"You know perfectly well what I mean." She frowned as a memory unfolded inside her mind. "Did you once have a big black cat with a white stomach?"

"Yeah. His name was Tuxedo because he also had a white ring around his neck that looked like a bow tie. Why?"

"I remember that you let me pet him once."

He didn't answer, but—lost in the memory—it took Kathryn a moment to notice the silence. She forced herself to laugh. "I didn't mean to get maudlin on you. It's funny I even remember such a little thing—I must have only been five or six."

"You were six," he said. "You'd just lost your first tooth. And it wasn't a little thing to you at the time."

She blinked in surprise. "You mean you remember it, too?"

"Sure I remember, because it was so unusual. Even before the kidnaping threat, you were never allowed to come into contact with the other kids on the estate. Afterwards, you were always so surrounded by nannies and bodyguards that we couldn't have gotten close to you even if we wanted to."

"And you didn't much want to, did you?" Kathryn asked softly. "I don't mean you personally, Jonah—I'm talking about all the kids. Nobody liked me. I'm sorry if it sounds like I'm whining, because I'm really not. It's just a fact."

"That nobody liked you? Nobody knew you well enough to dislike you, either. Look at it from the kids' point of view, Katie. You were the little princess, always clean and neat and curled and absolutely perfect. You can't blame a kid for thinking that you wouldn't be much fun to play with—even if we hadn't been threatened with our lives if we tried."

Kathryn frowned. "You were *threatened* into staying away from me?"

"In my case," he said levelly, "it didn't take much of a threat. I was six years older than you and I wouldn't have been caught dead playing with a little kid."

"But you let me pet your cat."

"That was different. As I recall, you looked at me with those enormous blue eyes and told me earnestly that you'd never had a kitty to pet."

"And you felt sorry for me," Kathryn said slowly.

"Of course I did. They never even let you out to run

in the grass, for heaven's sake. And there was probably a full staff meeting to assign blame when you reappeared with cat hair on your clothes.''

She was instantly concerned. ''Did you get into trouble?''

''No. They probably figured that the cat had been wandering around on his own, so they concentrated on keeping your leash tighter in the future. And you, silent little sphinx that you were, obviously didn't say a word, or I'd have been strung up from the weathervane for touching you. Katie, we'd better get busy or Jennie will fire us and we'll set a new record for shortest time on the job.''

''You don't have to help. I'm the one who volunteered.''

''What was Jock's philosophy again? Never turn down an opportunity to learn a skill? This will be good for me.'' He lifted the industrial vacuum cleaner off the cart and added ruefully, ''If only because tossing this thing around is like lifting weights. It'll build up my muscles so I can defend us both whenever Jock catches up with us.''

Even without a case of arthritis to make things more difficult, Kathryn soon understood why Jennie had put a limit on the number of guests at the motel. By the time she and Jonah had cleaned six guest rooms, Kathryn felt hot and sticky, her back ached, and her hands were chafed from wearing rubber gloves as she scrubbed. But she had to admit to a sense of satisfaction in standing in the door of a finished room, seeing the clear results of her hard work.

''Which is more of a reward than I get sometimes

from working at Katie Mae's," she told Jonah. "There's a lot of paper-shuffling in my job. That reminds me—you said something earlier about a prenuptial agreement. Do you think we should put our deal in writing, Jonah?"

He stopped struggling to disassemble the vacuum cleaner and looked thoughtfully at her. "Only if you don't trust me to give you half of all my worldly goods. Let's see." He began ticking items off on his fingers. "That means you'll be getting half of a wrecked pickup truck—between the insurance company and the salvage yard, we'll probably get a few dollars for it. Then there's half of a car that's still in a repair shop in Minnesota, but only if you also accept half of the bill for fixing it. And you'll get half of—"

"Don't be ridiculous, Jonah."

"You won't pay half the bill? Now in theory I agree that it's my responsibility, but I would never have gotten the ticket if I hadn't been helping you escape."

Half exasperated, she said, "I suppose you want me to pay half the ticket, too?"

"You already have," he murmured. "I took it out of our communal funds the first night."

The self-satisfied twinkle in his eyes made her smile, too, though a bit reluctantly. "Good. And I'll pay the whole repair bill, too, even though the taillights would have gone out no matter where you were, or who you were with. Now will you stop changing the subject, Jonah? You know perfectly well I'm talking about the fifteen percent of Katie Mae's I said I'd give you. If you want me to put that in writing, I will."

He looked at her thoughtfully over the power cord he was coiling. "You really want to see your father blow steam out his ears, don't you, Katie Mae?"

"It's none of his business."

"If he ever finds out that was a condition of the marriage, he'll soon make it his business. No, I think we'd better leave things as they are. Besides, we can't afford to hire an attorney, and anything we'd write up ourselves wouldn't be legal anyway."

"That's probably true," Kathryn said doubtfully.

Jennie knocked on the door. "I hate to interrupt, but how are you two doing?"

"Almost done," Kathryn said. She stripped off her rubber gloves and stuffed the last bundle of used sheets and towels into the laundry bag on the end of the cart. "There. I don't know how you do it, Jennie."

"Take one thing at a time and it's amazing what gets done—but I must admit I'm very thankful for the break you've given me today. I came down to ask if you'd join Sam and me for supper and maybe a game of Scrabble afterwards."

"If you tell me that you've spent the day cooking—" Kathryn threatened.

"No, dear. One of the women from my church circle brought over a casserole. She said it was because Sam's been ill, but I think she was really hoping to get a look at you two." She smiled mischievously. "So it would be unfair of us not to share the bounty with you. Half an hour? The casserole will be heated through by then. Let me take the cart back to the office, and you two go and get freshened up."

As they walked back to their room, Kathryn said, "I still think it would make sense to write it down. Just to make it absolutely clear that we're in agreement about this."

"Tell you what, Katie Mae. When the judge gets to

the part about 'with all my worldly goods I endow you' just wink at me, and we'll both know what you mean.''

She wrinkled her nose. "I don't think judges use that phrase. Only clergymen."

"Maybe if we ask nicely, this one will make an exception for us."

He dropped a kiss on the bridge of her nose, and with a sigh she gave up.

The casserole was delicious, the salad crisp and the hot rolls delicate—and Kathryn was perfectly sincere when she told Jennie it was the best meal she'd had in days. But Jennie and Sam were demons at Scrabble, and Kathryn and Jonah went down to a hard-fought but glorious defeat. Eventually they threw in their remaining tiles, laughing.

Jonah accused lightly, "I never thought you'd come up short where words are concerned, Katie."

"It would help if you weren't such a creative speller," she retorted and went to help Jennie with dessert and coffee. "Is there a Laundromat nearby?" she asked as they waited for the coffee to brew. "We're running rather short on clothes."

"Heavens, child, my washing machine runs all the time. Bring your things up and do them right here." Jennie didn't look up from the ice cream pie she was cutting. "And speaking of clothes, child—what are you going to wear for your wedding?"

It was a question Kathryn hadn't considered. "Jeans, I suppose," she said wryly. "That's about all the choice I have."

Jennie clicked her tongue sorrowfully. "And there's not much to be had here in town," she said. "It was such a shame when we lost our last dress shop, but that's the bad part of living in a small community—it takes a good number of people to keep those things afloat.''

And even if there was a dress shop nearby, Kathryn thought, there was still the small matter of money. ''I'll be just as married no matter what I'm wearing,'' she said, as much to herself as to Jennie.

''That's a very sensible way to look at it,'' the old woman agreed.

But Kathryn didn't feel very sensible. She couldn't help thinking with regret of the gorgeous satin and lace gown she had left stuffed in the bathtub when she'd walked out on Douglas. It wasn't that she longed for the dress itself; she could never wear it, for it would bring back too many memories of the luckiest day of her life....

Luckiest? she reflected, astonished at herself. What was she thinking of?

It must be the Scrabble which was still contorting her brain. *Unluckiest,* that was what she'd meant. Last Saturday had been the most devastating day she'd ever experienced. Discovering her fiancé's perfidy, and then realizing that her father was going to be of no help at all. Fleeing in panic, and then stumbling over Jonah...

But finding Jonah hadn't been unlucky. It had been the best thing that had ever happened to her.

Absently, she picked up the tray which held the dessert plates and followed Jennie back into the tiny living room behind the motel office.

''I've got the paint for the portico, too,'' Sam was saying, ''but my doctor won't let me climb a ladder yet. I wonder if you might find the time—''

''Sam!'' Jennie scolded. ''Stop hinting. Jonah has already done enough for us, without you trying to talk him into risking life and limb on a ladder.''

''I wasn't hinting, Jennie, I just mentioned it.''

''I'd be happy to paint the portico for you, Sam,'' Jonah said. His voice was warm and good-natured.

Other men might have agreed to do the work, Kathryn thought, though many of them would have done so with resentment, or in anger at being manipulated. But not Jonah.

She hadn't been confused at all a few moments ago, for it had truly been the luckiest moment of her life when she had stumbled over him in the driveway outside his father's cottage. Or perhaps the luckiest moment had come just a little later. Perhaps it hadn't been when she fell *over* him, but when she fell *for* him.

When she fell in love with Jonah Clarke.

CHAPTER EIGHT

THE mere thought shook Kathryn to the core, for falling in love was exactly what she had intended never to do.

She wasn't horrified at the idea of loving Jonah, exactly, for it really had nothing to do with him. Her discomfort wasn't because of him personally. It was the general idea that gave her pause.

Long ago, Kathryn had realized that for a woman in her position falling in love made no sense at all. Caring too much would leave her vulnerable, because it would make it possible for the man she adored to take advantage of her. To use her.

She'd proved that much with the Douglas debacle, she reminded herself. As it had turned out, only her pride had been wounded by her ex-fiancé's betrayal. Because she hadn't been silly enough to think herself in love, she'd remained clear-sighted, able to see his faults and failures. And when she'd discovered his true agenda she'd been able to act coolly, quickly, decisively. But if she'd made the supreme mistake of falling in love with him, she would have found herself listening to his explanations, believing his promises, forgiving his mistakes, even constructing excuses for him. And—probably—going through with the wedding.

She shivered at the thought.

No, she could not allow herself ever to be susceptible to that kind of blindness. It was far more sensible to keep feelings out of the matter entirely, to make lifetime choices based on good sense and logic instead of the irrational emotion called love…

And that, she thought in sudden relief, was exactly what she'd done. She'd made Jonah a logical and sensible offer, and he'd very logically and sensibly accepted it.

So, actually, this sudden brainstorm of hers was nothing to fret about. It had come long after their decisions were made, and therefore it had nothing to do with the agreement. Besides, she told herself, the notion of being in love with him was probably just a passing fancy, born of the fact that for days now she'd had only him to rely on. Once she'd returned to her usual world, she'd quickly get her detachment back. Everything would be all right.

And the bargain they'd made so straightforwardly would still be a logical and sensible one. Throwing it away because of a sudden crackpot conviction that she'd fallen in love with him would be foolish beyond words.

She let out a long, satisfied sigh, and realized that Jonah was watching her intently. ''Unless you have plans you haven't told me about,'' he said.

She had completely lost track of the conversation. ''I don't know what you're talking about.''

''Painting the portico,'' he explained patiently. ''Will it interfere with anything you've planned if I paint Sam's portico tomorrow?''

She shook her head.

He looked at her a bit oddly but turned to Sam. ''Then, weather permitting, it's a deal.'' He pushed his chair back. ''Katie's looking a bit glazed all of a sudden, so I think it's time for us to leave.''

She hadn't even noticed that while she'd been wrangling with her sudden insight, the other three had finished their desserts. Automatically, Kathryn murmured her thanks and goodbyes, and Jonah took her hand as they walked back down the length of the motel complex.

"What was going on back there?" he asked.

For an insane moment, she wondered what he'd do if she told him. He'd probably shriek and run, she thought, as horrified by the picture as she had been. They were pleasant companions, well on their way to becoming good friends. And that was the whole point. He wouldn't want a clingy, possessive, demanding wife any more than Kathryn wanted to be one. That hadn't been part of their deal.

"I'm just tired," she said. "I don't see how Jennie ever kept up with the cleaning if all the rooms were rented."

"The portico shouldn't take long, and then I'll help you."

A plaintive meow greeted them outside their room. "You have some nerve, asking where we've been," Kathryn told the kitten. "When I looked for you earlier, you were nowhere to be found."

Jonah pushed the door open.

"Two nights in a row in the same place," Kathryn mused. "I hardly know what to do. We'd better watch out, Jonah—we're getting set in our ways."

"I know. It's beginning to feel like home, complete with a house pet. I've even been tempted to hang up the fuzzy dice and really make it seem like ours. Go on to bed, Katie. I'll feed Sigmund Fraud tonight."

She watched as he filled the kitten's dish and carried it outside. Grateful to have a few minutes alone, she brushed her hair and teeth and turned off the lights except for a small one in the tiny kitchen area, then got into bed.

She hadn't realized quite how shaky she still was. Her stomach felt as if it was gone entirely. But then, that had been quite a blow she'd dealt herself—thinking for a few moments that she'd gone and ruined everything…

Jonah came in, moving quietly around the room. She feigned sleep as he settled beside her, arranging his pillow just as he liked it. Very soon, his breathing was quiet and even, and she opened her eyes just enough to take a peek at him.

Which was silly, of course. He was just Jonah. She'd looked at him a million times in the last few days. What could she possibly see this time that she hadn't noticed before?

In the dimness, his face was like an abstract painting, all angles and shadows and hollows. But her reaction wasn't at all the sort she'd have expected from looking at a piece of art, no matter how attractive it was. And she didn't feel the casual ease of familiarity as she surveyed him. Instead, an unexpected wave of tenderness rushed over her.

She had never felt anything in her life that compared to the aching need which consumed her now—the need to protect and comfort and cherish another person.

When she opened her eyes, she had expected to see the man who was her friend and ally and partner in flight. What she had seen, instead, was the center of her universe. The single most important person in her life. The one she would give her life to protect.

Eventually the nervous tension that had filled her settled into an uneasy calm as the truth she had been trying so hard to deny melted deep into her heart.

She had fallen in love with Jonah Clarke, and no matter how hard she tried to argue herself out of it, the feeling wasn't going to pass. It was too deep, too profound, too intense to go away.

If she had seen it coming, she might have been able to defend herself against it. But just as an untended vine in a garden wound itself tightly around and through a trellis until it was impossible to unravel it, her love for Jonah had sought out an opening in her heart and sneaked inside. And now it was far too late to uproot it. It had gathered too much strength, claimed too much territory, to be destroyed. The only thing she could do was accept what had happened.

Finally, in the light of her new understanding, things began to come clear in her mind.

No wonder she'd been so nervous last night about asking him to stay in Ash Grove and wait out the three days until they could be married. She'd been afraid, almost panicky, that when it came right down to the wire Jonah would realize that he didn't truly want to marry her, despite the sensible bargain they'd made. Afraid that their bargain wouldn't be as important to him as he was to her.

Now she could admit—to herself, at least—that the safety of a sensible marriage was not at all what she had been so anxious to achieve. Despite what she had told herself, despite all the sensible arguments she had constructed, that had never been her real goal. It was Jonah she had wanted, and only Jonah. She had simply been willing to go to any lengths—even to lie to herself—to get what she wanted.

Jonah—who was always willing to help where there was need, whether it was a scrawny kitten or an elderly and infirm couple. Or, she told herself wryly, a desperate heiress.

Marrying a fortune hunter to avoid marrying a fortune hunter... He'd been right all along; her argument had made no sense whatsoever, except in her own convoluted mind. What mental gymnastics she had gone through in order to create a scheme that was just barely rational enough to allow herself to believe it!

Now, of course, she understood what had really been going on. Within mere hours of joining up with Jonah, she had known in her heart that she wanted him for always. So she had manufactured an excuse which the logical half of her brain—the half which had very sensibly insisted that it would be foolish for her to ever fall in love—would accept.

Then, fully convinced that she was acting in great good sense, she had made her crazy offer, and he had accepted it.

So now what was she going to do?

Jonah gave a soft little snore, draped an arm over her, and pulled her close, curving his body around hers. Kathryn tensed, but after a few minutes, when he did nothing more than snore into her ear once more, she began to savor the warm security of his hold.

Surely, she thought, the answer would come to her, just as this knowledge had forced itself upon her. There was no need to act in haste.

Jonah was gone when she woke in the morning, and Kathryn had no difficulty in figuring out why. They hadn't turned on the air-conditioning, and the day was already uncomfortably warm for someone who was used to summer in northern Minnesota, where heat waves were few and short-lived. He'd no doubt decided to get an early start on the painting job.

In any case, she was relieved not to have to face him right away, and under intimate circumstances, because the night had left her with no more wisdom on how she should handle her problem.

What she ought to do, she supposed, was to tell him that she couldn't marry him after all. But Jonah himself had told her that he wouldn't accept any announcement of that sort without an accompanying explanation, and she wasn't at all sure she wanted to open that can of worms. She certainly couldn't tell the truth, for confiding to Jonah that she cared too much about him would make her just as vulnerable, whether she married him or not. She was only safe from the consequences of her folly as long as he didn't realize how foolish she had been.

It wasn't that she thought he would deliberately set out to manipulate her, as Douglas certainly would have. But in a way, that fact would only make it more difficult for Kathryn. Even a woman in love was capable of drawing the line where Douglas's brand of cold-hearted manipulation was concerned. But Jonah's sincerity would create pressure on her of an entirely different sort.

No, it was quite clear that she couldn't tell the truth.

There were other arguments she could use for not marrying him, of course—except that she'd done a pretty good job of demolishing all of them before they'd ever reached Ash Grove, so recycling them now would hardly be believable.

And if there was one thing she was certain of, it was that Jonah would accept nothing less than an iron-clad reason. Feeble excuses would get her nowhere.

Once I make up my mind to do something, he had

said, *I do it*. Cherishing that philosophy himself, he would no doubt expect that only something earth-shattering would have the power to change her mind about something which was really important to her. And that was a perfectly reasonable expectation, since she was the one who had come up with the idea in the first place. She was the one who had gone to enormous lengths to carry it out.

All of which left her squarely in the same muddle she'd started with.

Hoping that physical work would occupy her mind enough to let her subconscious gnaw on the problem, Kathryn pulled on jeans and walked up to the office to get the cleaning cart. High on a ladder at the front of the building, Jonah perched. Shirtless, with a wide paint-brush in one hand, he stretched catlike in order to reach the portico's high peak, stroking it gently with gleaming white paint.

If Kathryn had retained the vaguest of hopes that her revelation last night had been in error, her body's automatic reaction on seeing him would have turned that dream to dust. The rush of tenderness swept over her once again, but this time the reaction was muted by a competing emotion—for as she watched the lean hips, the broad shoulders, the muscles rippling in his bare back, her mouth went dry with desire.

Idiot, she told herself, *not to have expected that*. But she had been broadsided by the sensation—and it didn't take long to figure out why.

She had almost convinced herself, over the last few days, that her physical reaction to him was nothing out of the ordinary. A normal, healthy young woman, considering marriage, would of course not choose a man who repelled her. But she had told herself that there were many men she could choose from, any one of whom could satisfy her just as well as Jonah could.

Only now did she realize how wrong she had been. Nobody but Jonah would do.

How could she not have recognized what was happening to her, when his kisses melted her into a puddle? And why, feeling as she did, had she not thrown caution to the wind and made love with him?

Because you were afraid, a little voice in the back of her head mused. Not afraid that she'd be disappointed by the experience, of course, for she knew better. Instead, she'd been afraid—deep inside her where the truth had lurked, hidden away from the daylight—that making love with him would force her to admit that she loved him. Her restraint had been just another carefully crafted piece of denial. As long as she didn't discover how important making love with him would be, she could continue to believe in the illusion she had so carefully created—that she was marrying him only because it was the sensible thing to do.

She shook her head in astonishment at her own naiveté.

Jonah laid the brush down and, with paint bucket in hand, climbed down the ladder. "Good morning," he said. "Did you sleep well?"

She gulped, wondering why he was asking. Had she somehow given herself away? Perhaps she'd been suspiciously restless, or even—heaven forbid—talked in her sleep. "I thought I did," she said. "Why? Did I keep you awake?"

"No special reason for asking," he said easily. "Jennie's watching us from inside, by the way. I wouldn't be surprised if she's hoping for some kind of demonstration.''

Kathryn tried not to shiver at the thought, but knowing what was coming—how his kiss would affect her—made it difficult to stand still as he slipped an arm around her, to tilt her head back helpfully, to smile as his lips touched hers.

His mouth lingered as if she were made of rock candy and the longer he touched her the better she tasted. Kathryn could feel her temperature rising by the moment. The only way she could think of to keep from bursting into flames was to remind herself that, much as he seemed to be enjoying this, he'd had other reasons for initiating this embrace.

"And we must at all costs keep Jennie happy," she murmured against his lips.

He raised his head. "Yes, we must," he agreed. "Because she's making lemonade, and I'm dying of thirst."

Kathryn tried to push him away. He laughed and let her go.

The instant she was free she felt as if the fire he had fanned into life had suddenly been smothered by a bucket of water.

"Would you be a pal and go get me a glass while I'm moving the ladder?''

A pal. That was what he wanted, Kathryn told herself savagely. So if she was going to have him at all, that was what she would have to be.

Only later, after she'd handed up his lemonade and gone off with the cleaning cart, did she ask herself whether that almost automatic reaction meant that she'd made up her mind. Had she decided that she was going to have him, no matter what the cost?

* * *

Jonah repositioned the ladder so he could reach the end of the portico and climbed back to the top. But his mind wasn't on his work.

Kathryn was having second thoughts, that much was obvious. The way she had almost backed away from him when he started to kiss her—that was a new reaction, and he didn't think it was because she was sensitive at being observed. She'd kissed him so hesitantly that he wondered if she'd half expected him to toss her down on the sidewalk and make love to her right there.

Not that the idea hadn't crossed his mind.

Did I keep you awake? she'd asked. The question had sounded innocent, but it was also completely erotic. Could she possibly not realize the effect she had on him? Had it really not occurred to her that it was driving him crazy to have her in his arms and in his bed, but not be able to do more than steal the occasional kiss?

Perhaps it had been a mistake to let her have too much time to think about it all. Too much time to get cold feet. Fool that he was, he'd even asked her himself whether she was sure of what she wanted to do. More than once, he seemed to recall.

Well, it had been easy enough to say that he didn't want a reluctant bride. It was simply common sense— to say nothing about good manners—to make it clear that unless she was certain she was doing the right thing, he didn't want her to marry him at all.

But the truth was that it had been a whole lot easier for him to be a gentleman about Kathryn's choices *before* she'd started reconsidering their whole agreement.

Jennie and Sam had invited them for supper again, and afterwards mopped the floor with them once more at

Scrabble. "It's just because you're preoccupied," Jennie said, "with all the last-minute details to arrange."

Like what? Kathryn thought. They'd talked to the judge and set up an appointment for midmorning on Friday—just thirty-six hours off now. What else was there to do?

How different this was than the circus atmosphere surrounding the wedding she'd run away from. No fancy gown and veil to be fitted one last time, no Antoine to fuss with a dozen possible ways to do her hair, no ushers and bridesmaids to entertain, no platinum and diamond rings to have sized, no reception menu to need final approval...

She wondered idly if the real reason for all the traditions surrounding weddings was simply to keep the bride too busy to think. Without dresses and hair and attendants and rings and food to worry about, a woman had a lot more time to wonder if she was crazy to get married at all.

When they said good-night to Sam and Jennie, Kathryn turned automatically toward the far end of the motel complex, but Jonah hesitated on the step. "I think I'll walk over to the supermarket," he said.

Kathryn was startled. "Why? You can't be hungry after all the food Jennie pressed on you."

"No, I just want the exercise."

Before she stopped to think about it, Kathryn said, "Mind if I come along?"

He hesitated.

Kathryn almost withdrew the question. If he didn't want her...

She was opening her mouth to tell him she'd reconsidered when he said, "Of course I don't mind."

He sauntered along the sidewalk, hands in his trouser pockets, and Kathryn tried not to wonder why he hadn't even attempted to hold her hand.

Outside the supermarket she noticed a newspaper vending machine and said, "Do you have enough change to buy a paper? That's us on the front page—I think we should have a copy. Don't you?"

Jonah dug in his pocket and held out a handful of change. "At least, as souvenirs go, it makes more sense than your model of West Podunk."

Kathryn made a face at him. She picked a few coins from his palm, fed them into the machine, and pulled open the door. It was entirely ridiculous, she told herself, that her fingertips were still tingling from the fleeting contact with his hand.

The Ash Grove *Advocate* was both smaller and thinner than any other newspaper she'd ever read. The photo of their accident took up the majority of the front page. The damaged pickup was the most prominent feature; Kathryn had to squint to find herself. "And the clerk at the courthouse said this looked more like me than my passport picture does?" she murmured.

Jonah looked over her shoulder. "You look pretty yellow in the picture, but maybe it's the lighting out here. Want to split a bag of sunflower seeds?"

"No, thanks. You can have them all."

She leaned against a pylon and flipped through the newspaper while he went inside.

When he came back, he wasn't alone; Ash Grove's mayor had joined him. Larry Benson shook her hand and said jovially, "Why didn't you tell us?"

Kathryn shot a look at Jonah, but he only shrugged. "Tell you what?" she asked cautiously.

"That you two wanted to get married."

"I suppose we shouldn't have expected that story to stay under wraps."

"Not in Ash Grove," the mayor said. "Not much happens in this town that isn't considered news. Not that you're the subject of gossip, exactly. I heard it from the newspaper editor, who uncovered it at the courthouse when he picked up all the official records for publication."

"Publication?" Kathryn said faintly. Her gaze fell to the newspaper in her hand. She told herself it didn't matter, because there was less than no chance that Jock Campbell would happen to pick up the Ash Grove *Advocate* and read the courthouse news.

"The editor was just annoyed he didn't know about it in time for this issue," Mayor Benson went on. "He said he was going to call you, though, to ask if he could do a story about the wedding."

"No," Kathryn said.

"Sure," Jonah said at the same moment.

Mayor Benson looked from one to the other. "Well, you two can work that out, I guess. Just let me know if there's anything I can do to help."

"Maybe," Kathryn murmured as they started back toward the motel, "he'd loan us the fire engine for a getaway vehicle. What *are* we going to do, Jonah? To get home, I mean. Not only did we lose my credit card completely, but between the car repair and the cash advance we must have pretty much trashed yours, too. Maybe you should have taken that job at the body shop after all."

He strolled along in silence for a few moments, chewing on a sunflower seed. "Are you in such a hurry to get out of town?"

"Well, I'd rather not see a minute-by-minute description of the honeymoon on the front page of the *Advocate*."

"Then I'll see what I can do." He reached for another seed from the bag in his shirt pocket.

"What have you got in mind?"

"I'll let you know when I work it out."

"I thought we were going to share everything. Money, information—"

He looked down at her, eyebrows raised. "Did you really?" he asked politely.

Kathryn bit her lip. She could hardly argue about him not discussing the details of how they might get home to Minnesota, when she herself was holding back so much more than that. It was obvious that he realized she wasn't sharing everything; she only hoped that he hadn't figured out what it was that she didn't want to talk about.

When they reached the motel room, Jonah stopped outside. "Good night, Katie Mae. I'm going to sit out here awhile and finish my sunflower seeds."

She pushed the door open and felt warm, stale air rush out. "We forgot to turn on the air-conditioning again." She sat down beside him.

The sky was absolutely clear, and the lights of the little town were not powerful enough to wash out the stars. Kathryn sat with her knees raised, her arms wrapped around them. "I wish I'd learned the names of the constellations when I was a kid."

"What did you do with all your time?"

"Every minute of it was packaged and assigned. Jonah, what was it like to grow up there without the nannies and the bodyguards? I mean, you were cooped up on the estate, too. In a different way than I was, but still—''

''Not for long. Don't forget about the door in the wall.''

''How old were you when you found it?''

''Eight or nine, I suppose. It wasn't long after we came to live there. It wasn't as well hidden then, you know—and the security on the estate wasn't as tight as it was later, after the threat to kidnap you. So it wasn't quite as much a feat as it appears now.''

''Was it always just your father and you? I mean, I don't remember ever hearing anything about your mother.''

''She died about a year before we moved onto the estate.''

Kathryn looked down at her clasped hands. ''I'm sorry. You lost everything almost at the same time, didn't you? Your mother, then your home and your friends—''

''I managed. Being able to ramble all over the countryside helped a lot.''

''Didn't your father worry about you?''

''He figured I couldn't get into too much trouble without him hearing about it. But then, he didn't know I was going outside the walls.'' He picked a sunflower seed out of the husk. ''Katie Mae, are you going to back out of this wedding?''

She hesitated. This was it, she knew. She couldn't have asked for a better opening. He sounded more sad than anything else, as if he'd already anticipated the answer. Perhaps, because of that, he wouldn't even demand that she give reasons.

Tell him, she ordered herself. *Tell him that you can't marry him.*

But a rebellious little voice at the back of her mind suddenly asked why on earth she couldn't. *What,* it demanded, *was so different all of a sudden?* The reality hadn't changed one iota in the last few days—only her understanding of it had been altered. The fact that she hadn't been aware of the problem two days ago didn't mean it hadn't existed then. She just knew herself better now, that was all.

So here she was, standing at a fork in the road, and she had to choose which path to follow.

She could confess that she had done what she'd never intended to do—she'd fallen in love. But if she did that, they would both end up worse off. Jonah wouldn't have the Katie Mae's Kitchens stock she'd promised him, and she wouldn't have Jonah.

Or she could keep her secret, hug it close inside her heart, and keep right on loving him for all her life. If she married him, they'd both have what they'd bargained for; in fact, Kathryn would have much more. She would have the man she loved—just as long as she didn't tell him how much she cared.

What a tough choice, Campbell, she told herself wryly. Put it that way, and it was no choice at all.

"No," she said firmly. "No, I'm not backing out." She stretched her legs. "Ready to go in?"

"I'll think I'll sit here for a while longer."

"Oh." She felt confused, and then hurt. "Does that mean…" She stopped and tried to steady her voice. "Does that mean you were hoping I was going to call it off, so you didn't have to?"

"No," he said, and swore under his breath. "I can't

stand it anymore, Katie Mae. Having you curl up against me like that damned kitten. Not making love to you is taking every bit of stamina I have. But as long as you're not absolutely sure—''

"Who says I'm not sure?"

"Because what you say and what you do don't match up very well."

"Oh." She turned to face him. "Then maybe I need to change what I do." Her hand brushed his shoulder, crept up his throat, and came to rest at the nape of his neck.

"Katie." There was a catch in his voice. "You'd better think about this."

She tugged gently, until his mouth was only a whisper away from hers. "I've been doing nothing but thinking, Jonah. Now it's time to act."

CHAPTER NINE

AS HER hand brushed Jonah's skin, Kathryn noted that her fingers were trembling—not in fear but in anticipation. It seemed she had been waiting for this...for him...forever.

Maybe even before she knew him, she had been waiting—convinced that somewhere in the world was the right man for her. Waiting... until finally she had grown impatient and decided to settle for Douglas. But even after she had chosen him, something deep inside her had kept whispering that Douglas wasn't enough, that somewhere there was a better man, that she should have kept on waiting.

How else could she explain the unflattering swiftness with which she had believed the worst of Douglas? Even Jonah had protested that she hadn't given the man a chance.

She knew that she had been right about Douglas. There wasn't a shadow of doubt in her mind that he was the gambler and fortune hunter the usher had pictured. If she had needed confirmation, she would have found it in that conversation with her father on what should have been her wedding night—when Douglas had as much as admitted it. *We've both made mistakes,* he had said. Indeed!

But that had come much later; the cold fact was that she had not even given him an opportunity to defend himself before she ran. It hadn't even occurred to her to send her maid downstairs for Douglas—instead of her father—and to ask him about what she'd overheard.

She'd told herself that was because she didn't want to listen to excuses and explanations that she already knew she wouldn't believe. But that wasn't the whole truth. In fact, she had seized the usher's words as if he'd thrown her a lifeline, because subconsciously she had already known that she didn't want to go through with the wedding. Not because of Douglas—her apprehension had actually had very little to do with him personally—but because at the last moment she had rebelled against the idea of settling for less than the man she had dreamed of.

Her fingertips brushed Jonah's jaw, and the faint stubble of his beard reminded her that this wasn't some imaginary prince charming, perfect in concept but pale and formless in reality. This was Jonah—genuine and down-to-earth and indisputably real.

And he was hers.

She kissed him with the pent-up longing of all the time she had waited for him. Jonah groaned and pulled her closer—as if he was trying to absorb her, to make her a part of him—and Kathryn sank against him, every cell aching with desire.

Long before she was ready for the kiss to be over, he freed himself. She was still trying to articulate a protest when he stooped to pick her up, pushed the door open with his foot, and carried her inside.

"You said you weren't going to carry me over the threshold till after the wedding." Kathryn hardly recognized her own voice; it was low and husky and breathless.

Jonah didn't sound much more in control. "Standing in front of a judge is only a formality, Katie Mae."

And then there was no energy left for rational thought, no breath left for forming sentences. But there was also no need for anything more than the half-coherent murmurs of lovers as they explored each other and reveled in their union, reached for the ultimate fulfillment, and sank back to earth together in utter, exhausted bliss.

The sun was already high when Jonah woke, and Kathryn was still asleep. As he untangled himself from her embrace, she muttered something. A protest, he thought. Under ordinary circumstances it wouldn't have taken even that much to keep him beside her, but she sounded so sleepy and disjointed that he doubted she even realized she'd made a sound. He smiled and tucked the blanket closer around her before he went out to the pay phone in the parking lot.

It took a good deal of charm to sweet talk his way past Brian's secretary without giving his name. But finally he reached a frantic-sounding Brian, who demanded, "What in hell are you up to, disappearing this way?"

"It's Thursday morning, Brian," Jonah said reasonably. "When I talked to you on Monday night, you said nobody had even missed me."

"Well, a lot can happen between Monday and Thursday. There are an incredible number of people who are looking for you now. Most of them have blood in their eyes."

"Like who?"

"I'll summarize by category, if you don't mind, because I'd be hoarse by the time I recited all the names."

"That's okay, I can probably fill in the blanks. Hodges?"

"That's one of them. He's pretty anxious."

"A little uncertainty might be good for him. Look, Brian, I need you to do a couple of things for me." He rattled off the mental list he'd composed before he'd dragged himself away from Kathryn's side.

Brian was obviously writing things down, because he was silent for a moment after Jonah finished. "That's what you call a couple of things? Sure you don't want the moon, too?"

"That would be nice. Don't bother putting it on a silver platter, though." *Kathryn probably already owns a dozen of them.*

Brian uttered a strangled groan. "Dammit, Jonah, when are you going to be back?"

Jonah sobered. "Is Hodges really putting that much pressure on you?"

"What, you thought I was kidding? If you could get back here today—"

"Sorry. I have an appointment with a judge tomorrow morning."

"A judge? I suppose you got nicked for speeding or something. Can't you just pay the fine and get out of there?"

"Actually, this is shaping up to be a life sentence." He paused. "Stop gibbering, Brian, it was only a joke. I'll get back to work as soon as I can." He turned to lean his other shoulder against the pay phone and spotted Kathryn coming across the parking lot. "In the meantime, stall everybody. I'm counting on you, buddy."

He put the telephone down but he didn't move, just stood there and let his gaze run across Kathryn, from artfully tumbled hair to legs that he recalled as far and away too gorgeous to be hidden under jeans. It was too bad husbands weren't allowed to be dictators anymore, he thought. His first decree, the moment after the certificate was signed, would be that she could never wear anything but skirts from here on. Though, when he stopped to think about it, that would let every man in the world enjoy looking at her legs…

"Was that Brian?" she said as she reached the phone box, and he nodded. "Who's he supposed to stall? If my father's found him—"

"He didn't say anything about Jock." *Probably only because you didn't give him the opportunity, Clarke.* "My bosses seem to be getting a bit restive because I've disappeared."

"I didn't think they'd take the gone-fishing story seriously." She looked somber. "Oh, Jonah—don't worry about losing your job. There must be something at Katie Mae's you could do."

"Of course, if Jock fires you, it will be a little harder for you to pull strings to get me hired," he murmured.

"Then we'll go and lie on a beach somewhere while we figure out what to do next. We just have to get through tonight, Jonah."

With delight, he watched her turn pink as she heard what she'd said, and murmured in his best lecherous-villain voice, "I have a few strategies for that, my dear."

Kathryn finished cleaning the few rooms which had been rented overnight and had just started on their own when the telephone on the bedside table rang. She stopped dusting the model of West Podunk which was sitting on the bureau, and looked at the phone in horror. Four rings later she'd managed to convince herself that it must be a wrong number. No one could have possibly found them.

Unless it was Brian, she thought. If Jonah had told him where they were... But why would he have done that, knowing how tenacious Jock Campbell could be? No matter how much he trusted Brian...

She answered, and in utter relief heard Jennie's voice from the front office. "Kathryn, can you come up here for a minute?"

"Are you all right, Jennie?"

"I'm fine. Just come up to the office as soon as you can."

Kathryn threw her dustrag in the laundry bag, retied the red bandanna she'd used to restrain her hair, and sidestepped the cleaning cart parked outside their room. No wonder Jennie had known where to find her, she thought. She'd just looked out the front door for the cart.

In the office Jennie was hovering, wearing a conspiratorial air. "Sam and Jonah went to the hardware store and there's something I want to show you."

"If it's a mouse in a trap or a bat flying loose," Kathryn said warily, "it'll have to wait for them to get back."

Jennie smiled. "Neither. Come on in."

She ushered Kathryn through the living room and down a narrow hall to a bedroom which Kathryn hadn't seen before. Not much different in layout from the rental units, the room was obviously Jennie's; it was decorated with country quilts and wedding gowns...

Kathryn blinked and looked again. No, her eyes hadn't been deceiving her.

Dresses were hanging from the closet door, from the

curtain rods, from the tall mirror on the dresser. Dresses were laid out across the bed and draped over chairs. Some were white, others cream; there was even one in palest pink—but there was no question they were wedding gowns. Some were simple, others were drenched in lace and pearls. Some were street-length, some would touch the floor, and one had an elaborate beaded train that ran halfway across the carpet. There were more than a dozen in all.

"You're starting a bridal shop?" Kathryn said in bemusement, without taking her gaze off the dresses.

"You sounded so disappointed at being married in jeans." Jennie's voice was soft. "I wanted to offer you the dress I wore for my wedding, but then I thought, what if you didn't like it? I didn't want you to feel obligated to wear it anyway. But it was such a shame for you to have no choice in what to wear for your wedding. Then it dawned on me that if I was willing to share, others would be, too. It's that kind of a town, you see. So I just passed the word around, and the dresses came from everywhere."

Kathryn bit her lip hard, but the pain didn't stop the tears from coming. "Oh, Jennie—"

"Just a little gift from the women of Ash Grove. Now—what do you think? What would you like to try on first? We'd better get started, as we'll need a little time to make the necessary alterations."

"The brides wouldn't mind? I mean, I wouldn't dream of cutting anywhere, but we might need to take something in."

"Well," Jennie said with a smile, "the owners are done with them, aren't they?"

Kathryn pulled off her bandanna and used it to blot

mascara while she slowly studied each dress, circling the room to stand before each one. Finally she said, "This one," and pointed to a street-length ivory creation with puffy sleeves, a narrow skirt, and a lacy drape over the front of the bodice that made it look almost Edwardian.

Jennie helped lift the dress over her head, and watched as Kathryn turned in front of the mirror, smoothing the silky fabric over her hips. "It's perfect," Kathryn whispered. She met Jennie's eyes in the mirror and saw the way she was biting her lip. "Don't you think so? What's wrong?"

"Nothing at all," Jennie said. "That's my dress." She smiled mistily.

Kathryn hugged her, careful of the fragile fabric. "I guess you should have trusted your judgment in the first place. Sorry you had all the bother of getting the rest of the dresses."

"It was worth it, to see you choose. Now, you'll need shoes. I still have mine somewhere, I wonder if we could be lucky enough..."

Jonah and Sam had returned from the hardware store and were puttering around the front of the motel when Kathryn returned the cleaning cart to the office. She caught Jonah's eye as he was replacing a light bulb in the highest fixture under the portico. He smiled at her, and she felt her insides go as mushy as overcooked noodles.

He climbed down from the ladder and came toward her across the parking lot. "I brought you something from the hardware store."

She took the bag he handed her with some trepidation.

"I can't wait. A full set of screwdrivers? My very own roll of duct tape?"

"It's an unusual hardware store."

She peeked into the bag, and then exclaimed in delight as she pulled out a camera. It was a simple and inexpensive model of the use-once-and-throw-away sort, and the outside was emblazoned with "Happy Birthday" surrounded by bright balloons. But the thought touched her heart. "They didn't have one for weddings?" she teased.

"It was a close-out sale. If you don't want to use it for wedding pictures, maybe you'd like to get a shot of Sigmund Fraud to take home with you."

"Of course we'll use it at the wedding. We'll just have to find someone to actually take the pictures. And about the cat, Jonah—I've been meaning to talk to you about that."

"I don't believe I want to hear this."

"We can't just leave her here. There's no animal shelter to find a new home for her, because it's too small a town."

"So you want to take Sigmund Fraud home with you?"

"I know it will be a pain," she said hastily. "It's a long way to drive…if we're driving, that is. Do you suppose we could manage to rent a car?"

"It's too small a town," he echoed. "At the moment, I'm planning to borrow Cinderella's carriage. Katie, you have no idea how well the cat will travel. Surely Jennie—"

"Jennie's got enough to do. She doesn't need a cat to take care of."

"We may not even be able to catch Sigmund. She'll

hardly let me touch her yet. And if she's always been an outdoor cat, she's not going to take too well to being closed in.''

Kathryn knew he was right. But she bit her lip with regret.

Jonah swore under his breath. "When you look at me that way, Katie Mae, I'd swear you're six years old again and it's Tuxedo we're talking about. All right, I'll try to figure something out.''

She flung her arms around him. "I know you can manage it.''

"I said I'd try, Katie,'' he reminded. "But Sigmund Fraud may have other ideas, and she has claws.'' He drew her toward the sidewalk, pushing the cleaning cart out of the way of a car that had just turned in from the street.

The driver parked at a haphazard angle, blocking two marked-off spaces, and got out. She was a young woman, wearing the most elegant clothes Kathryn had yet seen in Ash Grove and carrying a canvas bag bearing the logo of a prominent Chicago specialty store.

A moment later Kathryn realized why the woman looked vaguely familiar. She'd been the driver of the Cadillac which had run the stoplight and wiped out their truck.

Kathryn stepped forward and offered a hand. "How nice of you to come and check that we're all right,'' she said. "I hope you're over any bad effects from the accident yourself.''

The woman glanced from the cleaning cart to the red bandanna tied around Kathryn's head to the oversize man's shirt—one of Sam's—that she was wearing. She didn't appear to see Kathryn's hand. "I didn't come to see you. I'm only here to drop something off for Jennie. So don't get any ideas that I came over to apologize."

"Or to do anything else that might imply you were taking responsibility for the accident," Kathryn murmured. "I'm sure your attorney would be proud of you."

The woman didn't seem to hear her. "So unfortunate for you, of course, to be reduced to cleaning motel rooms in order to have a roof over your heads. Or perhaps it was nothing new at all. Yes, considering the decrepit old truck you were driving, you must be quite used to that sort of thing. Where is Jennie, anyway? I can't imagine why she wants to borrow a pair of high-heeled brocade shoes, since she can hardly walk as it is, but here they are." She flourished the bag.

"I do hope they're not yours," Kathryn muttered. She'd sooner go barefoot than accept a favor from a woman like this one.

"No, my mother's. She has a million pairs. You know, I've just realized that you look really familiar. Now where was it I saw….in some magazine, I think. Or maybe it was a newspaper."

Kathryn froze. For a little while, she'd almost forgotten the newspaper story and picture about her flight. But the tale of the vanished bride was too good a story for newspapers anywhere to pass up, and Ash Grove, while off the beaten path, wasn't exactly cut off from the rest of the world. And this woman, with her designer clothes and brand-name tote bag, would be just the type to have noticed a story about a missing heiress…

Then Kathryn realized that the woman wasn't looking at her but at Jonah, and that her gaze had warmed considerably as she studied him.

Kathryn wasn't sure whether to be relieved or disgusted, but she had to smother the urge to snort. *What a line,* she thought. No doubt the next thing the woman said would be that Jonah looked just like her second husband, and then she'd coyly admit to having been married only once... as yet. The woman had enough nerve to pull it off, that was certain.

"I hear that a lot," Jonah said easily. "I think it's because celebrities so seldom bother to dress up or get haircuts anymore. It's not that I look like any of them, you understand, it's that they look like me."

The woman gave a trill of laughter. "I do love a man who has a good opinion of himself," she confided.

"Because it matches the one you have of yourself?" Kathryn asked sweetly. "If you'd like, I'll take that bag to Jennie. I have to go into the office anyway."

The woman handed it over without a second look. She was still eyeing Jonah as if he was a double dip of ice cream in her favorite flavor.

Kathryn escaped into the office with a sigh of relief. She parked the cleaning cart in its closet and went on through to the living room with the bag. "The shoes madame ordered have been delivered," she announced to Jennie, who was working on a quilt block. "Though, considering the messenger, I think I'll check the toes for poison darts before I try them on."

Jonah stopped in the doorway. "And I thought Sigmund Fraud had claws," he said with a note of awe in his voice.

Kathryn turned pink. "Sorry. I don't generally let myself go like that, but she got to me with that 'You look so familiar' business. Honestly—how transparent can a

woman be? I'm surprised she didn't try to take you home
with her.''

"Oh, she did,'' Jonah murmured. "But I told her it
wouldn't work because you'd be devastated if you didn't
have me to take care of, so she very kindly offered you
a job as the upstairs maid.''

Kathryn made a face at him.

"Does that mean you want some time to think it over?
I said we'd get back to her.''

Kathryn threw the shoes at him. He fielded them easily and tossed them back at her.

"Children who throw things generally need a nap,''
Jennie said calmly. "Run along now, both of you, and
have a good rest.'' She smiled sweetly and bent her head
over her needlework once more.

Kathryn's wedding morning dawned clear and warm. It
was hard to believe, she thought, that less than a week
ago she'd awakened on a different wedding morning.
Very different, indeed—she couldn't think of a single
thing that was the same.

Except the bride. And even that was questionable, for
Kathryn felt like a very different woman from the one
who had sat with feigned patience in front of a mirror
for more than an hour while Antoine fiddled with her
hair.

The only nerves she was suffering from this morning
were because of her fear that they might be late for their
appointment with the judge. Jonah seemed to be in no
hurry at all, but everything Kathryn tried to do seemed
to soak up twice as much time as it ought to. It was even
taking longer than usual to get hot water in the shower.

"Tell you what,'' Jonah offered as she adjusted the

water temperature. "We could be ready faster if we shared the shower."

"Only if we didn't take our clothes off," Kathryn said absently.

"Katie Mae, you have such a delightfully dirty mind. All I said was—"

Kathryn shut the door in his face.

When it was Jonah's turn to shower, she hurried to dry her hair, then gathered up her makeup and scribbled a note for him. *Meet me at the office. Jennie's going to fuss with my hair.*

"And other things," she said under her breath.

Jennie was waiting with the ivory dress ready to drop over Kathryn's head, and she'd even found the saucy little hat that she'd worn on her own wedding day. It took a little time to get it settled just right, but it was worth it, Kathryn decided as she looked at the image in the mirror.

Jonah seemed to think so, too. His long-drawn breath when he caught sight of her was a better compliment than anything he could have said.

"Stop staring at each other and come on," said Sam impatiently. "I don't want to speed on the way to the courthouse. It wouldn't be respectful somehow."

"Then let Jonah drive," Jennie told him. "He's perfectly capable."

"Except he'd be watching Katie instead of the road. Can't say as I blame him, either. Come along now, all of you."

But Sam couldn't have gotten his car out of the parking lot if he'd had a platoon of National Guardsmen to help. Parked along the street in front of the motel, blocking the drive, was a row of vehicles, including Ash

Grove's fire engine and single police car. The high school's marching band was standing in loose formation, instruments at rest, and a team of flag-waving girls on horseback was holding a last-minute rehearsal. In the center of the parade was a white horse-drawn buggy with high wheels and red upholstery.

"I guess you weren't kidding about borrowing Cinderella's carriage," Kathryn said.

Jonah shook his head. "Don't look at me. I didn't have a thing to do with this."

Mayor Benson bustled up to them, beaming and holding a megaphone in one hand. "What do you think? It was my idea."

"I never doubted it for a minute," Jonah assured him.

"Actually, it gives us a little extra practice for the Fourth of July parade," the mayor confided. He raised the megaphone. "Into line, now, everybody! Let's go!" He waited while a small girl in a taffeta dress presented Kathryn with a sheaf of flowers, and then bowed her to the carriage. "You mustn't expect too many people waving from along the route, now."

"I won't get my hopes up," she promised.

The mayor offered a hand to help Jennie into the carriage, as well. "Because most of them are already down at the courthouse waiting. They didn't want to take a chance on getting caught in traffic and missing the wedding."

Kathryn dissolved in giggles, and she had barely regained her composure by the time the parade moved six blocks and stopped in front of the courthouse. Even then she had to take a deep breath and not look directly at Jonah as he lifted her down from the carriage, or she'd have gone off again.

The courthouse didn't smell of dust and old books today; instead, the scents which greeted them as they came through the front door were of ham and barbecue sauce and cinnamon—a delicious hodgepodge of aromas which reminded Kathryn that in her hurry she'd missed breakfast entirely. "Is there a cafeteria here?" she asked.

Jennie shook her head. "No, that's the church ladies arranging your reception. Since there isn't a trial going on, they decided to use the big courtroom for a potluck."

"You knew about this?"

Jennie drew herself up to full height, and then smiled. "Well, not *all* of it."

The clerk who had taken the application for their marriage license came down the stairs so fast that it seemed to Kathryn that she hit only every third step. She looked pale, and a filament of dread twined around Kathryn's heart. "The judge just called," she said breathlessly. "He's holding an emergency arraignment in the next county, and he's running awfully late."

"And I was worried about being on time?" Kathryn threw up her hands. "It figures. Nothing else has gone smoothly, so why should that?" As she turned, her gaze fell on the mayor. "Mayor Benson, I don't suppose you—"

He shook his head regretfully. "Sorry, but mayors aren't allowed to officiate at weddings."

Jonah said, "As long as everything else about this wedding has been backwards, maybe we should keep the streak going and hold the reception first."

"Great idea," the mayor said cheerfully. "And we can give you the key to the city while we're waiting. Crank up the music, over there. Champagne, anyone?"

*   *   *

The first hint that the judge had arrived was when the decibel level in the courtroom fell dramatically, but the confirmation for Jonah was when he noticed that everyone who was holding a champagne glass suddenly but discreetly moved it out of sight.

"Hello, everybody," said a short, round man whose official black robes made him look just a bit like a cannonball with arms. He looked thoughtfully over the crowd and focused on Kathryn and Jonah as if he'd recognized them. "Well, let's get on with the business of the day." He didn't look at Mayor Benson as he added, "And after that's done, Larry, you can pour me a glass of that…um…grape juice you're all drinking."

"Happy to, Judge," Mayor Benson said.

Jonah glanced at his watch and then out the courtroom window at the street below, where the parade vehicles were still parked. He took Kathryn's hand and followed the judge through the crowd to the end of the room.

And he wondered what could be taking so long.

Her hand felt small and cold in Jonah's comforting grip. Now that the moment was here, Kathryn had to admit to a good case of nerves. Maybe her father had been right after all, and brides always did suffer last-minute anxiety attacks. Goodness knew if she'd had real doubts, she wouldn't be standing here. The events of this week would have been enough to drive the most self-assured bride to the edge of panic. If none of the obstacles they had faced so far had made her call off this wedding, then a last-minute case of the shivers wasn't going to, either.

The judge raised his voice. "Gather around, everybody."

At first, the noise of the crowd shifting inside the

courtroom almost drowned out the commotion in the hallway outside. But as everyone got into place, Kathryn began to hear the sound of feet hitting stairs, of hurried steps in the corridor.

"What's that?" she said, but her throat was so tight that she hardly made a sound.

Jennie, standing beside her, looked toward the doorway and said calmly, "I rather imagine it's your father, dear."

Kathryn gulped. "Who—how did you know that?"

"Oh, most everybody in town knows," Mayor Benson said.

"Not that anyone would have snitched on you," Jennie assured, "because we all think it's just too romantic."

"But if nobody here in town called him," Kathryn whispered, "then how did he find us?" She turned to Jonah, looking for reassurance.

His brown eyes were steady, his hands holding hers were firm. But he didn't say anything.

The double doors of the courtroom burst open, and Jock Campbell came in. As always, he was surrounded by an entourage, and Kathryn ran an eye almost fearfully over the group. But Douglas wasn't there. At least that was one blessing.

Jock cleared his throat. "Well, Kathryn, it appears I'm still in time to put my two cents' worth in before it's too late to change your mind. Sorry to cut it so fine, Jonah, but you forgot to warn me that I might have trouble finding ground transportation after we landed at the airport. Do you know how far away that is, my boy?"

CHAPTER TEN

IF THE courthouse had crumbled into dust around her, Kathryn couldn't have been more shocked. She stared up at Jonah in disbelief. "*You* told my father?"

"Yes," he said. "But things got a little out of hand. I didn't intend it to happen like this."

"I'll just bet you didn't," she said, her voice low and hard. "You didn't anticipate the parade, and you didn't expect the judge to be late. So what *did* you have planned, Jonah? That Jock would come bursting in just a little too late to stop the wedding, so you could gloat? The gardener's son marries his daughter, and there's not a damned thing he can do about it?"

Jonah's face tightened as if she'd slapped him.

Kathryn's stomach roiled. She knew as she said it that the accusation was an insult, the kind of low blow that she was ashamed of delivering—but in the midst of her own disillusioned anguish, she couldn't stop herself. "Just breaking it to him after the fact wouldn't have had quite the same kick, I suppose. It wouldn't have been nearly as satisfying as letting him see for himself what you'd accomplished."

He didn't answer. He wasn't even looking at her.

She was hurt that he hadn't even tried to defend himself—as if he believed what she thought of him was totally unimportant, not even worth trying to justify. "You lied to me, Jonah. All those phone calls you said were to someone called Brian were to my father instead, weren't they? Your bosses were getting restive—what a tall tale!''

"It wasn't a lie, Katie." Jonah's voice was level. "There's really a Brian, and he really does work with me. In fact, he's right over there."

Half blindly, she followed his gesture to a young man who was standing near Jock. He didn't look as if he fit into her father's usual entourage, however. Unlike the members of Jock's staff, who wore their dark blue suits and understated ties as if they were uniforms, Brian was wearing khakis and a denim shirt.

Suspicion trickled through her. "If he works with you, what's he doing with my father?"

"Since I didn't ask him to come," Jonah said calmly, "I'm not sure how they happened to team up."

"Maybe he worked out some kind of deal for himself while he was acting as go-between and reporting back to Jock."

Jonah shook his head. "Don't blame Brian for any of that. I was the one who called Jock."

Kathryn felt half sick at the idea that he would defend Brian, but not himself.

Her thoughts were swirling wildly. *None of this makes sense,* she told herself. If Jonah had simply wanted to gloat to Jock, why wouldn't he have waited till the wedding was over? Or even the honeymoon? Watching Jock sputter ineffectually would surely be more entertaining if the pleasure were to be drawn out at length. And there was no doubt in Kathryn's mind that after a week or so of the kind of passion she and Jonah had shared in the past couple of days, she would have gone home in a blind stupor of satisfaction, unwilling to listen to a word against her handsome husband.

That sort of revenge might not have quite the same explosive impact as an encounter at the very foot of the altar, but she was certain it would have been much longer-lasting and therefore more satisfying. Surely the last thing Jonah would have done was to take a chance that her father would move faster than expected or the wedding might be delayed, allowing Jock to interrupt and stop it altogether.

That, however, was precisely what had happened. But it was impossible, she told herself, that Jonah—the strategist who had so carefully considered every move during their flight—hadn't seen that possibility and made allowances for it.

So—if it wasn't simply gloating that he'd intended, what had been in his mind?

Had he wanted Jock to interrupt the wedding? But that made no sense, either. Nobody—certainly not Kathryn—had been holding a shotgun to his back in order to force him to the altar...

Jock had finally made his way across the crowded room to them. Automatically, Kathryn turned her head to offer him her cheek, but she didn't smile or greet him.

"Hello, sweetheart. I see I'm still on your most-unwanted list." He kissed her lightly. "Perhaps it will help when I tell you that Douglas has been forbidden to set foot on Campbell property again, and also that he was escorted out of the headquarters of Katie Mae's Kitchens by two armed guards."

"Then he was embezzling, along with everything else." It was nothing more than an idle comment, made because it seemed to be expected of her.

Jock's eyebrows went up, and he sent a look at Jonah as if to inquire whether she could really be so unmoved.

"It appears he was only getting started. He had apparently been holding off on tapping that resource until he was pretty much sure of you. I owe you an apology, my dear, and my thanks for the timely warning."

Kathryn nodded. "I accept."

"So now that you've made your point and been proved right, there's no more need for this melodrama."

Melodrama wasn't a bad description of the ups and downs of the last week, Kathryn decided. Even now, she felt a little as if she were tied to a railroad track with a train bearing down—and no hero in sight.

But surely it was odd that Jock had chosen that particular word. How much did he know about the last week, anyway—and exactly how had he learned it?

As if you need to ask, she thought drearily.

"Anyway," Jock said, turning to Jonah, "Thanks for taking care of her, and for keeping her from going off the rails entirely. I'm sorry you weren't able to get through to me on Monday night, by the way, but it's your own fault." He chuckled. "You sent me on a wild-goose chase from Wisconsin to Nevada. That was clever—dropping hints at a gas station where you'd be certain to be overheard. I was burning up the lines from the plane, so nobody could call in. By the time the command center realized how important your call was and paged me, you'd hung up."

Monday night, Kathryn reflected. After she'd suggested staying in Ash Grove, but before they'd even gotten a marriage license, Jonah had called her father. And, when he hadn't been able to reach Jock in person, he had kept quiet about the attempt and indulged her by going through the motions. Pretending that he wanted to marry her. And very convincingly, too, she thought miserably, remembering the difficulty over her lack of a driver's license and the way he had searched for her passport....

"In that case," she said curtly, "I'm only surprised it took you so long to get here, Daddy."

"Oh, I didn't find out where you were till much later." With a nod of thanks, Jock took the glass of champagne the mayor offered him. "Jonah didn't want to divulge that information until he found out what state of mind I was in and that I wasn't going to come after him with the militia for running away with my daughter. And since I couldn't call him back anywhere, we ended up communicating through my little wireless e-mail gadget, and it took a while to work out all the details. But once I found out you were safe, Kathryn, then it was really just a matter of getting here before the wedding."

"You sound as if you think there's actually going to be one." Kathryn's words cut through the hushed room, bringing gasps from the crowd.

"Kathryn," Jock said uncertainly. "Sweetheart, not *again.* You really can't make a habit of this, you know."

"You said yourself that there was no need for the melodrama anymore."

"And there isn't. I came down here mostly to make sure you weren't doing something you might regret."

Like sleeping with him? she thought. *You were too late, Daddy.*

"Like getting married just because you were mad at me," Jock went on. "It wouldn't be a very good foundation for a life. But when I walked in and saw the way you were holding on to each other..." He pointed.

For the first time Kathryn realized that her hands were still nestled in Jonah's. She pulled away. After his warmth, the room-temperature air felt as if she'd immersed her fingers in a tub of ice.

"You couldn't do any better for yourself," Jock went on.

"Oh, really?" Kathryn said curtly. She looked up at Jonah. "Sorry about the fifteen percent of Katie Mae's you thought you were going to get. I guess you'll just have to live without it, but I'm sure you'll manage—a man with your fertile brain must have all kinds of opportunities." She shot a glance at her father, wondering if that little tidbit would change his attitude toward Jonah.

Jock choked on his champagne. "Why would he want it?"

Kathryn stared at him.

"I mean, really, sweetheart, he could buy us both before breakfast." Jock reached into his pocket and pulled out what looked like a cross between a cell phone and a remote control. "I figure—not that it's any of my business, of course, Jonah—that this little e-mail gadget I love so much has made you a couple of hundred million already."

"Not personally," Jonah said.

"Close enough, when you own the whole company," Jock mused. "Having an electronics firm in the family would be a nice diversification, Kathryn. If you could see your way to—"

The greatest electronics genius of your day, she had called him. She'd meant it sarcastically. But...it was *true?*

Behind Kathryn, the judge cleared his throat. Kathryn jumped six inches. She'd forgotten he was there.

"I think this discussion has gone far enough, and a

little privacy is called for," he said. "If you'll come with me to my chambers." Jock moved as if to follow him, but the judge fixed him with a steely gaze. "The bride and groom only, please."

If someone had offered her a choice between following the judge or having each individual hair plucked from her head by the roots, Kathryn would have taken the new hairstyle. But she could think of one thing that would be worse than explaining it all to the judge, and that was standing in a roomful of Ash Grove's citizens, the people who had done so much for her in the past few days, and confirming that she was indeed a fool and that there would be no wedding. She might as well have thrown their generosity back in their faces.

The judge's chambers were small, barely big enough for a desk and a couple of chairs. He closed the door firmly behind them, shutting out the sudden babble of voices rising in the courtroom. "I'll give you half an hour alone," he said firmly. "I suggest that for the sake of your future peace of mind you use this time to come to some agreement. You will notice that there are two doors out of this office. One of them, of course, goes back to where the mob's waiting. The other leads past my private office to the back stairs and the side entrance of the building. If either or both of you choose to take that exit instead of proceeding with the wedding, tap on the door of my office, and I will break the news to the people in the courtroom."

He went out into a narrow corridor.

"Nice idea," Kathryn said. Her voice shook only a little; she was proud of herself. "Going out the back door, I mean. Except we'd have to steal a car for the getaway." She caught herself too late. "I mean...two cars.'' She faced Jonah, her arms folded across her chest as if to keep herself warm. ''If you didn't want to marry me, all you had to do was say so.''

''You've got it all wrong, Katie Mae.''

''*Don't* call me that.''

''You told me I could call you anything I wanted.''

''Yeah, and you said we'd share everything fifty-fifty. You could have told me, Jonah. You didn't have to go to such lengths and create a circus if you wanted out.''

''I didn't call your father because I wanted out.''

''Oh, you *did* want to marry me?'' she said sarcastically. ''What a convincing demonstration you've offered!''

''You wouldn't even talk to him, much less give him a chance to apologize for not believing you about Douglas, or even to tell him you were all right. So I called him. I wanted you to be certain that you weren't acting in anger or desperation.''

She shook her head. ''I don't believe you. You've been making a fool of me all week. Pretending, going along with the game, playing the spy. Such a shame it's too warm to wear a trench coat—you'd no doubt have enjoyed it even more if you'd had the proper costume!''

''I don't blame you for being angry, Kathryn.''

The use of her formal name sent chills through her blood. How she would miss the companion who had so unmercifully teased his Katie Mae.... If he'd ever been real at all, she thought, and not just another figment of her imagination.

''You have a nerve,'' she said. ''Pretending to be a line worker, putting circuits together for some electronics company—''

''You assumed that. I never said it.''

She reconsidered the conversation and decided that he was right. But the deception was no easier to take just because it had been a silent subterfuge instead of an active lie.

"You could have told me you *were* the damned company," she snapped. "No wonder you didn't want to sign an official prenuptial agreement. You'd have had to disclose everything you owned. Or did you think I already knew and I was after your money?" She shook her head, trying to clear it. "This is all so confusing I don't even know where I stand."

"I should have told you about my job, yes. But you were so set on marrying a fortune hunter—"

"That you decided to be one? How perfectly flattering!"

"What it comes down to," Jonah said, "is that I was afraid of what you might do if I didn't. You were so upset—at Douglas, at your father—that there was no predicting what direction you might jump. Your whole line of so-called logic about why it would be smart to marry a fortune hunter was idiotic, but the dangerous part was that you really believed it. So I figured it couldn't do any harm for me to act the part. As long as you thought I fit the description, you'd be satisfied—and you'd have some time to cool off and reconsider before you did anything you couldn't back out of."

"So you decided to protect me from myself."

"Damn right I did. I asked what you'd do if I turned you down, remember that? And you told me you'd just go find someone else."

"I didn't mean it, Jonah."

"You'd picked me up quickly enough," he reminded.

"That was different."

"Different how? Because I was the gardener's son, so I'd been properly indoctrinated through the years and I could be trusted not to take advantage of Miss Kathryn?"

"*No.*" Anguish rang in her voice, she knew. But she couldn't possibly explain what had really happened. That she had recognized him as her soul mate, but had been too stupid to admit it even to herself. That she had made her crazy proposal only because she was already in love.

"I couldn't just turn you loose," he said. "In that self-destructive frame of mind, you might have done anything at all."

No, I wouldn't, she thought. *If I couldn't have you, I wouldn't have wanted anybody.*

"So you called my daddy," she said bitterly. "But he wasn't there, so you strung me along while you waited for him. You gave me all the trappings, didn't you, Jonah? A marriage license, an appointment with the judge…" She swallowed hard. "Even a wedding night and a honeymoon."

After a long silence, he said heavily, "I'm sorry if you regret what we shared."

She couldn't answer. Even in the midst of her pain, she knew that when the agony eased, she would hold on to the memory of their time together. She might not cherish it, exactly, because cherishing was for pleasant memories. But she would clutch it tight and make sure that she never forgot the brief span of time when the man she loved had been hers.

"I'm sorry for it all." He turned toward the door. "Shall I send your father in right away or would you like a little time to yourself first?"

He's leaving. Though why should she care? "You mean you're not going to sneak out the back way as the judge suggested?" she asked carelessly.

Jonah's jaw tightened. "No, I'm not going to take the cowardly route. Someone has to face all those people and apologize, but there's no reason for it to be you. It wasn't you who messed this up so badly."

"Yes, it was. It was my idea in the first place."

"We're not going to argue about it, Kathryn. I'll take the blame. There's no need for you to have that pain to bear, too."

His hand was on the doorknob when she said quietly, "That's what it comes down to, doesn't it, Jonah? That's what it all comes down to."

He paused. "I don't know what you mean."

"You feel sorry for me, having to face all the lovely people out there whom we've hurt. But that isn't all. You've always felt sorry for me, haven't you? That's why you let me pet your cat, back when I was six years old. And to you I've always been poor little Katie—the one who didn't have friends, who couldn't take care of herself, who was so self-destructive she might just pick up the first tramp she ran across. That's why you helped me get outside the walls in the first place. That's why you played along with the marriage scheme." Her voice was rising. "And that's why you made love to me, isn't it? Because you felt sorry for me!"

He said something under his breath. Then he wheeled around and came toward her. In his eyes was a glint of anger that she'd never seen before, and it took her breath away.

In the tiny room, there was nowhere to run. Kathryn backed up against the desk, her hands braced on each side of her. "Let's just forget I said it, all right?" Her voice quavered.

He stopped less than six inches from her. "Is that really what you think? That I made love to you out of some kind of pity?"

Unable to deny it, she gave a jerky nod.

Jonah reached out with both hands, letting his fingertips rest gently against her temples, cheekbones, and jaw. The pad of his thumb moved softly over her lips in a caress as low and sensuous as a kiss.

Kathryn's lips parted as she panted for breath.

"Yes," he said softly, "I did feel sorry for you at first, when you were trapped on the estate and you didn't know how to get away. Then when you came up with your screwball plan I was exasperated at you, and concerned that you'd actually do it. And then...then I felt this." With a single swift movement he pulled her away from the desk and into his arms, and he was kissing her with a ferocity that left her knees the consistency of mashed potatoes. Her tiny hat seemed to get in his way, and he pulled it off in order to thread his fingers through her hair and hold her closer yet.

She gave a little whimper of longing, but he seemed to think it was a protest and released her abruptly. She leaned against the desk, fighting to keep her balance, and her breath came in a small, shaky sob.

Jonah's voice was suddenly gentle. "I'm sorry. That was not at all how I intended to behave."

"It's quite all right." Her voice was taut. "Don't let me keep you any longer, Jonah."

"I haven't convinced you, have I?"

"Not entirely. In any case, it doesn't matter. I'm quite aware that you have spent the last week cursing the impulse that made you choose that particular day to visit your father.''

''I've cursed quite a lot of things in the last few days,'' he admitted, ''but that wasn't one of them. If I hadn't been there, you couldn't have fallen over me, and none of this would have happened.''

''That's exactly the point I was making,'' she said acidly, and paused. ''You mean...so what *do* you mean?''

''I don't consider it a wasted week, if that's what you're asking. Oh, honey, why do you think I was there that day, anyway?''

The answer was so obvious that it had never occurred to her to wonder about it. ''You were visiting your father.''

''You think I would have actually chosen to visit him on the one day when he was frantic all morning because every flower petal and blade of grass on the whole estate had to be perfect, and tied up all afternoon with a wedding and a reception that I wasn't invited to?''

It didn't make any sense, now that she considered it. ''I didn't think of that—how much extra work it was for him, I mean. Besides, you could have come to the wedding. And it was a weekend. You'd have had Sunday with him...''

He said, very deliberately, ''I drove up from Minneapolis that morning, and I was planning to go back that evening.''

''But I don't understand. If he'd told you about the wedding—''

''He told me, all right. That's why I came. Only I didn't come for the wedding. I came to attend a wake.''

She was confused, and it must have showed in her face.

"I came," he said gently, "because it was the best way I could think of to force myself to face the fact that you were married."

"Why should you care?"

His smile was a little twisted. "Why, indeed," he said, "when you didn't even know I was alive…. Because, my dear, when I was twenty-three I was home from college on winter break, and I saw you leaving the house one night wrapped in a white fur, with your hair spread out across the collar. And for the first time I realized that you'd grown up."

"Girls generally do," she said.

"You were a fairy princess—and a young man's dream. Of course," he added meditatively, "after that, you were more like a splinter in my finger."

Quite a sudden drop from fairy princess, she thought.

"You were always there," he said. "Like a tiny, almost-invisible splinter. Most of the time you didn't cause me anything but mild discomfort, but once in a while—mostly whenever I saw you—you'd sting like fury. Even all these years later, every time I caught a glimpse of you it was like being twenty years old again and watching my fairy princess."

She rubbed her temples. "I don't get it. Didn't you ever even try to bump into me, Jonah?"

He sounded surprised. "Of course not. I was in love with a dream—I knew it wasn't real. It couldn't ever be real."

Her heart twisted with regret. But it all made sense. He certainly hadn't been in love with *her,* because he hadn't even known her, only the fairy princess of his dreams.

"There have been a fair number of women in my life," he said, "but none I've been seriously interested in. None of them could compete with my fairy princess."

"That's a pretty unfair standard, Jonah."

"I knew it made no sense at all to keep on thinking of you, but I did it anyway—until my father told me you were going to be married. And that's why I was on the estate that day. I was going to say goodbye."

Without ever having said hello? she wanted to ask.

"It was like cutting out the splinter, you see. I knew it would hurt like hell to do it, and it would have been easier to ignore it for a while longer. But slicing open the finger is the only way to make the wound heal. So I came on your wedding day because I knew that I had to see you married and happy before I could get on with real life. Maybe even get serious about one of those other women."

Kathryn sighed. "How ironic that instead, I walked right over you. And so you were the gentleman and saved me from myself."

"That was the original intention, yes." His voice was dry.

"I suppose I should thank you. Or maybe you should thank me. Because one thing's certain, Jonah. After spending a week with me, you surely must be over the whole idea of the fairy princess."

He smiled a little. "It didn't take long to realize that you weren't exactly the girl of my dreams."

She'd tried to add a little levity, but now she regretted

the impulse. "Right. Spare me the details, if you don't mind. I can imagine them perfectly well."

He didn't seem to hear. "Because the real Katie," he said softly, "was a thousand times more than the fairy princess could ever be. Because this time I didn't fall in love with an image, or with a dream, but with a woman."

Her breath caught in her throat, but caution reasserted itself as she remembered that he hadn't acted much like a man in love. "And it scared you so much that you called my father to rescue you."

"It scared me, yes," he admitted. "Because I wanted you so much that I knew I couldn't trust my judgment to do what was best for you. And I was afraid that if you married me because you were hurt over Douglas and angry with your father, that we would both pay a hell of a price. But I didn't call Jock to rescue me. I called him to rescue you, before you did something you couldn't live with. And I was right, wasn't I?"

"If you mean you think I regret making love with you—"

"This morning you were rushing around as if you were headed for an execution instead of a wedding."

"I was not!"

"It looked to me as if you were grimly determined to go through with it because you thought it was too late to do anything else. I was planning to tell you on the way over here that Jock was due any minute, that it was all right to change your mind. But I didn't know about the parade, or the reception, and suddenly there wasn't time. People were lined up to talk to you. Jock was running late, the judge was ready…" He paused and drew a deep breath. "I want more than anything in the world to marry you, Kathryn. But only if it's what you want more than anything in the world, too. So I guess it's time—''

"To go find the judge and tell him we're ready," Kathryn said softly.

Jonah had stopped dead. "Katie?" He sounded as if someone had kicked him squarely in the stomach.

"We're a perfect pair. You're a masochist and I'm an idiot. You set out to save me even though you knew it would hurt you horribly, and I tied myself into knots to keep from admitting that I'd fallen in love with you—''

Then she was in his arms, and there was no more need for words.

Kathryn didn't know how long the judge stood in the doorway before they noticed him, but he was smiling. "Shall we go and interrupt the celebration?" he said, and led the way.

In the courtroom, Larry Benson was telling Jock about the accident that had introduced them to Ash Grove. "Actually had to cut them out of the truck," he said earnestly. "It was a good thing I'd just sharpened my pocket knife that morning."

Jock looked bewildered but game. He obviously suspected that he was having his leg pulled, and he was eager to change the subject. "I haven't had a chance to get a good look around, of course," he said, "but this town—what's its name again?—seems like a good site for a Katie Mae's, so if you're interested—''

Jonah caught Brian's eye. "I think you have something for me," he said.

Brian stopped looking at Kathryn long enough to dig into his pocket and pull out a small, square velvet box.

"My mother's rings," Jonah said. He opened the box.

"I thought they'd work for now. Later we can get whatever you want."

"I want these," she said softly, without looking at them.

Jonah caught his breath and kissed her.

"No more of that," the judge said. "Not for a few minutes, anyway."

Brian said, "I thought you told me there was no woman involved in this caper."

"You asked if she was a blonde, a brunette, or a redhead, and I said none of the above," Jonah reminded.

"Oh," Brian said. "Right. I'll remember that dodge in the future."

"Don't bother. You won't ever need to ask again. Perhaps I should introduce you—Katie, this is Brian, who's the administrative genius who makes my business run smoothly. Which reminds me, why are you here? I told you to put that box and my passport on the plane and send it down, I didn't tell you to come along."

"I thought maybe we could talk about Hodges."

"Later. You'd better ask your buddy Jock if you can hitch a ride back as far as Minneapolis, because I'm taking the jet."

"Cinderella's carriage is a jet?" Kathryn asked softly.

"Only a little one," Jonah said. "Not as elaborate as your father's."

"Where are you going now?" Brian howled. "Hodges is going to have a first-class fit if you don't make an appearance. He keeps saying the stock is going to tank if Wall Street finds out how unpredictable you are."

"We're going back to the motel, where we will pack up Katie's souvenirs and corral our new cat, and then we're off on our honeymoon—wherever my bride wants to go. Though if you wouldn't mind making a side trip, Katie, just long enough to soothe my board of directors…''

Kathryn laid a finger across his lips. ''Darling,'' she said, ''for you…'' She smiled and whispered, ''I'd even skip the plane and drive to Nevada.''

From boardroom…to bride and groom!

A secret romance, a forbidden affair, a thrilling attraction…where a date in the office diary leads to an appointment at the altar!

Sometimes a "9 to 5" relationship continues after hours in these tantalizing office romances…with a difference!

Look out for some of your favorite

Harlequin Romance®

authors, including:

JESSICA HART: Assignment: Baby
(February 2002, #3688)

BARBARA McMAHON: His Secretary's Secret
(April 2002, #3698)

LEIGH MICHAELS: The Boss's Daughter
(August 2002, #3711)

HARLEQUIN®
Makes any time special ®

This Mother's Day
Give Your Mom
A Royal Treat

Win a fabulous one-week vacation in Puerto Rico for you and your mother at the luxurious Inter-Continental San Juan Resort & Casino. The prize includes round trip airfare for two, breakfast daily and a mother and daughter day of beauty at the beachfront hotel's spa.

INTER·CONTINENTAL
San Juan
RESORT & CASINO

Here's all you have to do:

Tell us in 100 words or less how your mother helped with the romance in your life. It may be a story about your engagement, wedding or those boyfriends when you were a teenager or any other romantic advice from your mother. The entry will be judged based on its originality, emotionally compelling nature and sincerity.
See official rules on following page.

Send your entry to:
Mother's Day Contest

In Canada
P.O. Box 637
Fort Erie, Ontario
L2A 5X3

In U.S.A.
P.O. Box 9076
3010 Walden Ave.
Buffalo, NY
14269-9076

Or enter online at www.eHarlequin.com

PRROY

Do you like stories that get *up close* and *personal*?
Do you long to be loved *truly, madly, deeply...*?

If you're looking for emotionally intense, tantalizingly
tender love stories, stop searching and start reading

Harlequin Romance®

You'll find authors who'll leave you breathless, including:

Liz Fielding
Winner of the 2001 RITA Award for
Best Traditional Romance
(The Best Man and the Bridesmaid)

Day Leclaire
USA Today bestselling author

Leigh Michaels
Bestselling author with 30 million
copies of her books sold worldwide

Renee Roszel
USA Today bestselling author

Margaret Way
Australian star with 80 novels to her credit

Sophie Weston
A fresh British voice and a hot talent!

Don't miss their latest novels, coming soon!

HARLEQUIN®
Makes any time special®